In danger

My heart is pounding. My stomach is doing major flip-flops. I feel everyone must know what I have in this bag. What if someone on the streetcar sees what I'm doing and turns me in? What if some German stops me, just to harass me, just to scare me, and looks in my bag?

Other Scholastic books by Carol Matas:

In My Enemy's House
Greater Than Angels
Cloning Miranda
The Garden
After the War
Jesper
Daniel's Story
After the War
The Lost Locket
Adventure in Legoland
Safari Adventure in Legoland
More Minds (with Perry Nodelman)
Of Two Minds (with Perry Nodelman)

Lisa

Carol Matas

Scholastic Canada Ltd.

Scholastic Canada Ltd.
175 Hillmount Road, Markham, Ontario L6C 1Z7

Scholastic Inc.
555 Broadway, New York, NY 10012, USA

Scholastic Australia Pty Limited
PO Box 579, Gosford, NSW 2250, Australia

Scholastic New Zealand Limited
Private Bag 94407, Greenmount, Auckland, New Zealand

Scholastic Ltd.
Villiers House, Clarendon Avenue, Leamington Spa,
Warwickshire CV32 5PR, UK

Canadian Cataloguing in Publication Data

Matas, Carol, 1949–
Lisa

ISBN 0-590-24189-3

1. World War, 1939–1945 — Denmark — Juvenile fiction.
I. Title.

PS8576.A7994L5 1994 jC813'.54 C93-095180-8

First published by Lester and Orpen Dennys Limited, c/o Key Porter Books Limited, Toronto, Ontario.

10 9 8 7 6 5 Printed in Canada 9 / 9 0 1 2 3 / 0

For Per,
with love and thanks

ACKNOWLEDGMENTS

First I should like to thank my husband, Per, without whom this book would not have been thought of. He was my guide to Denmark through the research and the writing and was always there with moral support. I am also indebted to my mother-in-law and my father-in-law, Inge and Olaf Brask, who took the time to tell me their stories. I wish I could name every Dane who, with kindness and generosity, sat with me and told me about the war. I should like to thank them all, and most particularly the wonderful people of the B'nai B'rith of Copenhagen and Chief Rabbi Melchior.

For both its financial and its moral support I thank the Jewish Foundation of Winnipeg, which gave me grants to begin my initial research and backed the project when I most needed the help; also the Manitoba Arts Council and the Ontario Arts Council, whose financial support made it possible for me to take the time to write this book; also Perry Nodelman and Sara Parker, who gave me invaluable encouragement.

Finally, I wish to thank Janet Hamilton, who edited the book with great sensitivity, and Louise Dennys, who understood and supported my work and helped me make this the best book I could.

CONTENTS

FOREWORD

In 1939 Europe was locked in a tense confrontation between the "Allies"—Britain, France, and three other countries—and the "Axis"—Germany and Italy, ruled by the aggressive Nazi and Fascist governments of Adolf Hitler and Benito Mussolini, respectively. Germany had already overrun Austria and Czechoslovakia, and many people believed that all of Europe was threatened, but the leaders of England and France still hoped for a peaceful solution.

On September 1, 1939, the German army suddenly attacked Poland. With this strike against their own ally, Britain and France had no choice: both declared war, and most of the Commonwealth—including Canada—followed suit.

On April 9, 1940, the German army invaded Denmark and Norway. Denmark fell within the day; Norway resisted but was conquered within a month. These countries, and eventually most of Europe, became "occupied" lands—controlled and exploited by the Germans and able to fight back only in secret, through highly dangerous "resistance" movements, until the Allies (now joined by the United States) finally won the war in 1945.

Lisa

ONE

A Buzzing in My Ear

I have lots of time to think now. There's nothing else to do. Just think and wait, and wait, and wait. Of course, I know some of the people here. But no one wants to talk. They're all thinking about themselves, I guess. They're thinking, "Will I make it?" So many images flash through my mind . . . but certain ones stand out more than others.

I remember I was dreaming about a bee. A giant bumblebee. It was buzzing in my ear; it was going to sting me. I opened my eyes and sat up with a start, but the buzzing didn't stop. Oh, great! I thought I'd grown out of that a long time ago. You know those dreams you have when you're a kid—when the big bad wolf is chasing you, and you wake up and it's still chasing you.

Your eyes are open but it's still there, and you can't get off the bed to get help because each way you look that wolf is suddenly in front of you. . . . Finally you make a break for your parents' room and safety, and end up at the kitchen table drinking hot chocolate at four in the morning. But I'm twelve now. A little old for—

"David! David, wake up." I can hear my mother's voice. She's calling my father. Why?

I'm not at my best, or should I say my sharpest, at six A.M. But it finally dawns on me that I'm not dreaming. I jump out of bed and run to where Mother is standing at the living-room window.

My father comes up behind me and puts his arm around my shoulder. He peers out the window. We're on the second floor of a four-story apartment house that faces the street and the lake. We have a pretty clear view of this part of Copenhagen. Across the lake are more apartments. The sun is rising, throwing shafts of blue and green into the gray water, but it's all mixed up with the black shadows of airplanes. Row after row of planes roars overhead, flying low so we can see their markings clearly.

"Germans," Father says quietly.

I get a cold shiver right down my back. I look at Father's reflection in the windowpane, but I can't make out his expression. I'm now almost as tall as he is. He's so small, so delicate. Why couldn't I take after him? But, no, I'm big, like Mother. Not fat, just tall and lanky, with big bones and lots of wavy auburn hair. And freckles! And green eyes. I'm like my mother in every way but one. She's so graceful she just glides through life. Not me. I have my mother's bigness and my father's clumsiness. Wonderful combination.

"Oh, God," I hear her whisper.

"What is it?" My brother Stefan is staggering into the room. Well, it takes an enemy invasion to get him up in the morning. I decide to keep the crack to myself, though.

My mother tells him quietly, "It's German planes."

Stefan runs over and turns on the radio. It's hard to believe, but Denmark has just surrendered. The radio announcer reads a message from our government. They tell us that life will go on as usual, with Parliament ruling, the king still heading things up. . . . I go away from the window and sink into a chair.

Stefan is yelling and screaming. "Surrendered! We never even tried! We hardly fired a shot! Should we all go out there and lick the Germans' boots now, too?"

He looks as if he's going to cry. I haven't seen him cry since he was about eight and I was six and I stabbed him in the hand with my fork because he stole my piece of pastry.

His face is all red, and he's stamping his foot.

"Throwing a tantrum won't help," I mutter. It worries me to see my older brother behaving this way—as though he's out of control.

He glares at me. "That's about all that's left for us, isn't it? We don't get to fight. We just roll over and surrender. And if we throw tantrums we'll all get sent to our rooms—except this time the rooms will have bars and locks, and Mommy won't come to let us out." He looks me in the eye.

I make a face at him, but my heart isn't in it—he's scaring me. My mother puts on the kettle.

"I guess there won't be any school today," I say, thinking, well, at least there's one good side to all this. We're having a math test today that I didn't study for. Instead, my best friend, Susanne, and I went to the bakery and bought cream puffs and lay on the floor of my room stuffing our faces and reading our new movie magazines.

My mother looks at me calmly. "Go get dressed, Lisa. The radio hasn't said anything about people staying home." Then she looks at Stefan. "You'd better walk with her today. I don't want her on the streets by herself."

Stefan nods.

"I can take care of myself," I object—but not too strongly, not so that she'd change her mind. "I'm not afraid of those . . . those gorillas."

"No," says my father quietly, "but you should be."

Well, that shuts me up. We get dressed. I try to eat some cheese and rye bread, but everything seems to stick in my throat.

"Come on," says Stefan, "let's go." Like Father, Stefan's small. I'm almost his size already. He has Mother's hair and Father's white skin. And someone's blue eyes—Grandfather's, maybe? I can't really see him helping me out if a German wants to shoot me, but I go with him anyway. He's so upset that he stomps out our front door without his book bag. I run back to the kitchen to get it, figuring that's easier than trying to say anything to him. Mother is slumped over the kitchen table, her head in her arms, crying. Father has a hand on her shoulder. I stop, thinking maybe I should do something, say something, but Father motions me away. I see his eyes are all red, too. I run after Stefan, who's already downstairs waiting for me in the foyer. I hand him his bag. He grabs it without a word and pushes open the front door of the building as if it were a German soldier.

We walk quickly down our street and turn down Ourøgade. We walk along the narrow sidewalks, down the narrow street. Yellow brick houses connect with red brick ones, their copper roofs green with age. Then we're on Jansvej, big, gray-stone apartment buildings lining the streets, and shops at street level. Everything seems normal. Kids are walking to school, people are going to work, shops are opening. What did I expect? Everything to look different? But now we start to see trucks driving by, and they're filled with German soldiers. And then there are pieces of paper floating everywhere, German airplanes flying overhead—yes, the papers have just been dropped by the airplanes. I bend over and pick one up. It's all written in terrible Danish, with some German and Norwegian thrown in. It talks about how Denmark is threatened by England and France, especially by that warmonger Winston Churchill.

"You see, Lisa," says Stefan, his voice dripping with sarcasm, "the Germans are here only to *protect* us. The Germans are keeping us free from an invasion by France and England. Aren't we lucky to have such good friends?"

I don't answer him. I feel sick inside—the papers, the soldiers—Germans riding down our streets waving guns—I can't believe it's happening.

We meet our cousin Erik on the way. He's thirteen, and he and I are good friends. He falls in with us.

"So what do you think?" I say, throwing the leaflet on the sidewalk in disgust.

"About what?"

"About what? About what?" I say. "About . . . do you think Gustav Wied is a good writer? Or do you think he's overrated?"

"Well . . ." he replies thoughtfully. He thinks he's such a brain, and he is.

"No, come on now," I say, "seriously." Stefan is rolling his eyes in disbelief. "About the Germans. What do you think?"

Erik shrugs. "I don't think things will be much different. Dad says we just have to keep our noses clean and everything will be okay."

I hear Stefan hiss under his breath, "That's right, Erik. You be a good little boy."

For a minute I think Stefan is going to let Erik have it. He hates him anyway. Erik claims he isn't Jewish. His parents let him choose, and he just got confirmed last month as a Lutheran. Stefan doesn't think you can choose whether or not to be Jewish. You just are. Not that our family is terribly religious. But we light the candles on the sabbath, and we go to synagogue on the High Holidays, and, well, I guess I like being Jewish. I'm sort of proud of it. After all, we get eight days of chocolate at Chanukah, and if you're Christian it's all over in one day. And Father always brags about the accomplishments of our Jewish ancestors.

Erik and I have never really talked about what the Nazi party is doing in Germany. Still, I'm surprised now to hear him so unconcerned. But his parents aren't interested in politics, while Father reads to us from the newspapers every night. So maybe, for once, Erik just doesn't know enough about things.

"Haven't you heard what's happening to the Jews in Germany?" I ask. "The papers say their schools have been shut down, their businesses have been taken over, and the Jews themselves are actually disappearing. They're taken to big camps, then never heard from again. Our parents are worried sick about Cousin Isaac—aren't yours? No one's heard from him in three years."

"That's because he's a Communist," Erik retorts. "The Nazis hate Communists. He's probably in jail. I bet we'll hear from him soon."

"But don't you believe any of this?"

"I think some people will believe anything," Erik says. "But it's just a bunch of rumors so far."

At this point Stefan, who is walking by my side, moves over so Erik is between us. Then he casually sticks out his foot. Erik falls flat on his face.

Stefan keeps walking, and he calls to a couple of his friends up ahead, "Hey, there's this rumor going around that Erik tripped on his way to school. I don't believe a word of it, do you?"

Stefan's friends slow down and wait for him. I can hear them laughing; then they all start to talk at the same time about whether or not we should have fought the Germans.

The rest of the way Stefan walks with his friends, just ahead of Erik and me. I'm mad at Stefan, but Erik is not acting all that bright either. I mean, I don't think the newspapers would print rumors. And Father and Mother believe it's true.

"We can't just ignore the Germans, you know, Erik," I say. "This isn't their country. They have no right to be here."

"Well," he says, laughing, "Dad says at least the trains will run on time."

"It's not funny," I snap. "I don't know how you can laugh about it."

We get to school, and my teacher, Mrs. Jensen, tells us that we all have to try to cooperate and not make trouble and stay calm and then—then she sort of runs out of steam and sits down and starts to cry.

We're all really embarrassed, and no one speaks, and Susanne and I spend the whole day writing notes to each other about how we'll blow up all the Germans we can, if we get the chance. What we still have to learn is, you make your own chances.

TWO

Just an Idea

"I can't do it! I won't do it!"

I can hear my father's voice, low but insistent. I am trying to sleep, but I haven't been able to. Every time I shut my eyes, all I can see is German soldiers. I tried to think of something nice so I could sleep. I thought of my father and me sailing on the sound last September. The sky was so blue, cloudless, the sea cold, bracing. We went with friends of Father's, on their boat: Dr. Niels Knudsen, the surgeon, and his wife, Tove, and their daughter, Inge, who's just a year younger than I. I felt so happy, the wind blowing in my face until my skin tingled, the sun cool but bright, the grown-ups laughing and clowning, Inge and I trying our best to help sail. . . .

I don't sleep well at night; it's too dark. We were

ordered to put black blinds up on all our windows so no light would filter through at night. That's so the Allied bombers won't be able to find their targets. They say the German patrols shoot at any window with a bit of light showing. Anyway, my parents think I'm asleep, but I can't help overhearing. I guess I could help going to my door and pressing my ear against the keyhole. But I don't.

"What will you do? Tell them to their faces you won't treat them?" my mother asks, her normally calm, deep voice sounding sort of squeaky.

"Yes!" exclaims my father. "Right to their goddamned faces!"

"You'll go to jail," my mother says. "You'll be shipped off because you're Jewish. We'll never see you again. You'll go to work at the hospital one morning, and we'll never see you again."

All of a sudden I'm cold, my teeth are chattering. And I'm terrified. It's funny. That first day, the day of the invasion, everyone seemed to know what to feel except me. Stefan was mad, my parents were worried, even scared, Erik couldn't have cared less—and as for me, well, it all just seemed so confusing, so unbelievable.

Anyway, that was in April, right before Passover, and there was so much to do that I didn't have time for too much thinking. I helped my mother clean the Passover dishes, Stefan did the floors, and we got everything spotless. We stocked up on matzohs and threw out all the bread and locked anything else that had leavening in it into a special cupboard. I guess locking the cupboard is a habit left over from when Stefan and I were little and we used to raid it for cookies.

We invited Erik's family to the Seder dinner. Adam, Erik's father, is my father's second cousin, and they come every year. They're our only family in Copenhagen. Uncle Poul and his family live up in Jutland, too far away to come. The Knudsens were invited, too, and Stefan's friend Jesper. For Christmas and Easter we get invited to the Knudsens', or I go to Susanne's and Stefan goes to Jesper's, so it all works out great.

Passover has always been such a wonderful holiday. But this time, as we were passing around the bitter herbs to remember how bitter it was for the Jews to be enslaved in Egypt, Stefan said, "Now it's happening all over again. We're slaves again. Only this time, when we have to leave Denmark, it won't be like the Exodus. There won't be anything to celebrate."

"Stefan," said my mother, her voice warning and pleading at the same time.

"Will it?" he continued. "No, it won't be the promised land. It'll be concentration camps. And death."

"Now, just a minute, young man," objected Adam, Erik's father. "Don't you go adding to all those wild rumors. There's no proof the Jews in Austria and Germany are being pushed around. And anyway, here in Denmark we still have our own government. We're in control!"

Well, it was just a big mess after that. Stefan got into a fight with Cousin Adam. All anyone could talk of was the war, the Germans. It was awful.

I had practiced the four Seder questions, and I asked them well, but no one even noticed or complimented me or anything. I was furious—at Stefan, at the Germans, at everyone.

But all that was a week ago. Now it's two weeks since the invasion, and now, now I'm not stunned, I'm not angry, I'm just scared.

All those conversations Father and Mother and Stefan had at dinnertime are coming back to me: how the Nazis hate Jewish people and blame them for everything. I can't understand that. Here there's no difference between anyone. We're all Danes, and that's it.

We can't even read about what's happening anymore. Father has stopped reading the papers to us because they're all controlled by the Germans. They're nothing but propaganda. He says we won't have a free press until the Germans leave. But Radio Free Denmark broadcasts through the BBC in England and says what's happening, so we've started listening to the radio every night.

"I can't help that!" It's my father's voice again.

It's strange about my father. He can't sit at the table without knocking something over, or walk without tripping, but he's considered one of the best surgeons at the hospital. I always wondered where he got the courage to go to medical school—I mean, being so clumsy. He just says he wanted it too badly to give up on himself. I bet he makes his patients pretty nervous when they see him spilling ink containers and bumping into his desk. They must think, my life is in *his* hands?

"No!" My mother is adamant. "It won't work. It won't accomplish anything. If you feel you can't treat them—"

"How can I?" he interrupts. "One of them comes to me with an upset stomach from overeating *our* Danish food, or a bullet wound because one of *our* people was brave enough to try to do something, and then I'm supposed to fix him up? Why? So he can ship me off to some camp next week? So he can kill that same freedom fighter next time?"

"No," sighs my mother, "you're right, you shouldn't. But if you don't . . ."

Suddenly I have a brilliant idea. Forgetting that I'm eavesdropping and should be sleeping and will probably get murdered, I throw open my door and spew it all out.

"Father, Father, I've got it! You should keep on treating them, but treat them wrong. Be very nice, but don't do stuff right."

Slowly the anger fades from their faces. They look at each other. My father has a very pale, thin face, surrounded by dark curly hair. Some color now returns to his cheeks, and he actually smiles.

"Yes," agrees Mother. "Just give them sugar pills, anything."

Father looks at her.

"I have an oath. To medicine." He pauses. "But I'm a Dane." He talks slowly, almost to himself. "Not enough to kill anyone. No. Just enough to keep them in bed. Put them out of commission. Painkillers that are really sleeping tablets. Headache pills that will give them stomachaches. It's not much, but it'll do until I can find a way to really get them."

Suddenly they're both looking at me. I know it's just dawned on them that I should be asleep, that I was listening.

"I'm sorry," I say, as I back up into my room.

My father winks. "Don't make a habit of it," he says, "but you may have just saved me from going crazy. At least now I can do a little something."

I nod, shut my door, and crawl back into bed. What can *I* do to fight the Germans—a big, gawky twelve-year-old who isn't particularly brilliant at anything? Maybe Stefan will know. I'll ask him first thing in the morning.

Then something hits me. Maybe my idea hasn't been such a good one. Maybe the Germans will find out what Father's doing and take him away, and it'll be all my fault. But it was just an idea. Does just having an idea mean someone could die? Now I realize how different everything really is. My teeth start to chatter again. I slide under my quilt, but I can't sleep for a long time.

THREE

Stefan and Jesper

I'm sitting in class, trying not to stare at the clock, waiting for the school day to be over. I have a plan. I'm going to follow Stefan today.

I know he's up to something. I overheard him and Jesper having a big fight two nights ago. Mother and Father were out; the boys were sitting at the kitchen table. My door was open a crack, and I could hear perfectly. Eavesdropping is starting to become a habit.

Jesper said, "Look, my contact says that the resistance doesn't want Jewish people in dangerous situations, situations where they can be caught. The Germans will only use that as an excuse. 'See, here we have Jewish saboteurs. Now you see why we have to round up the Jews and send them away. They threaten the very peace of Denmark.'"

"So you want me to just sit here and do nothing?" Stefan growled.

"Not me, Stefan, the resistance—and some of them are Jewish. They don't want to take any more chances than necessary. But they need people for the underground printing presses. You could do that."

"So the Jews are supposed to keep quiet and not make trouble?" Stefan objected. "That did them a lot of good in Germany." I could hear him push back his chair; he paced the room. "Don't you see, Jesper? There *is* trouble. We're not making it; we're trying to help unmake it. No, it's up to us to fight, any way we can. There will be lots of people for the presses—not so many for the other work. And if you have to lie to your superiors, lie. Or just don't tell them I'm Jewish. I don't care. But I'm going to work along with you."

Jesper sighed. "You're right," he said. "I agree with you. If the Germans want an excuse to round up the Jews, they'll make one up. They don't need real evidence." Jesper had pushed his chair back, too. "I'll talk to them, Stefan. I'll tell them it's both of us or neither of us. I'm not going to lie. I'll make them listen."

After that I started thinking and I realized that, in fact, everyone in my house was acting strangely. But no one admits to a thing. Father stays out until all hours. I know because I wait up, just to be sure he gets home all right. I stare into the dark until I hear the outside door open and close softly. And Mother, well, she seems to be doing her regular things—going to the university to teach English, always back by the time I'm home from school—but I don't know, I have this feeling. . . .

It's been over six months since the Germans came. They're everywhere. On every city block there are pairs of them out on patrol, or rows and rows of them parading down the street. Sometimes, when there are just two of them, Stefan and I play chicken. We walk straight for them, talking, pretending not to notice them, and see who moves aside first. Often they do, but sometimes they don't, and then I think Stefan carries it too far. He'll walk right between them. Once one of them hit him, right in the side, with the butt of his rifle. That didn't stop Stefan; it just made him more determined. But with SS men or the Gestapo, even Stefan doesn't play chicken.

I'm almost thirteen now, and I want to do something. Playing chicken is just not enough. I'm not stupid; I know people are doing things. Sometimes I find leaflets on the streetcars, telling the news from the war—the real news about what's going on. One I read described how Norway fought the Germans, really fought, and destroyed a huge part of Germany's navy. So even though Norway ended up occupied, just like us, they made a big difference in the war and really helped the Allies. Another leaflet described how three factories were blown up right here in Copenhagen, factories that made things such as boots and radio parts that helped the Germans. And another was all jokes and cartoons about the Germans. I'll bet they hate that the worst—being laughed at.

Someone must be printing the leaflets, getting them out. I asked Stefan, but he said I'm too young and I'm a girl. Well, I'm as big as he is—bigger, actually—and he's lucky I didn't flatten him. I could, but I don't, out of pity. And, of course, there's the small chance that he's stronger than he looks. He can be pretty fierce when he gets mad.

At last, the school bell. I've got to get out of here before Stefan leaves his school in the building next door. I run out just in time to see Stefan and Jesper turn the corner in the direction of Østerbrogade. At first it's easy to follow them because there are so many other kids on the street. I just stay behind the crowd. But after a while most have gone home and the streets are getting empty. Now it's only them, me, and a couple of others walking. If Stefan and Jesper turn, they're sure to see me. They seem to be heading toward the children's playground. I decide to take a chance and get there another way.

I turn down Classensgade and end up in the playground. I hide behind a tree and see them coming the other way. They're looking around now, really casually, but I can tell they're checking to see if anyone is around. A man is walking in from Stokvej. He has a big coat on. It's November, and damp and cloudy and pretty cool, but he's dressed for winter. He sits down on a bench. When he gets up, he's left a large package behind. Jesper and Stefan sit down on either side of the package. I notice they're wearing their long winter coats, too. They're doing something, shoveling the contents of the package inside their coats. Now they're walking away. They're heading out of the park. They walk practically right past me, back to Østerbrogade, and wait for the streetcar. They get on.

What should I do? They'll see me if I get on, but if I don't I'll lose them. I decide to make a run for it. But I'm too late—the streetcar moves away and I'm left standing there. I can see Stefan looking at me through a window, his face all crinkled up and worried.

I realize that if I run really fast and cut through the park, I may be able to catch the streetcar two stops ahead. I've got very long legs, and when I want to run I can really move. I get to the stop, panting, a biting pain in my side, about half a minute before the streetcar. I try to look really calm as I get on and sit down. I look around for Stefan, but I can't see him. Then there's a tap on my window, and he and Jesper wave to me from outside as the streetcar moves away. They're laughing. I jump up and start to call Stefan the worst, the dirtiest name I can think of—when I notice everyone is looking at me. I sit down. A freedom fighter has to learn control. So I bite my nails.

Then I see it. On the floor. A small piece of folded paper. I'm sitting alone in my seat. I look across the aisle; no one is looking at me. I reach down slowly, pick up the piece of paper, slip it in my pocket. Then I get off the streetcar at the next stop.

I'm about eight blocks from home now. I hurry. The paper feels as though it's burning in my pocket. I reach our building, throw open the door, slip across the waxed foyer floor, then take the steps two at a time. I rush into the apartment and into my room, slamming both doors. My mother calls to me from the kitchen, "Lisa, is that you? You're late." I open the note. Yes, it's a bulletin from the resistance. They've managed to blow up a tool factory and some rail lines. They tell us to listen to Radio Free Denmark for more information.

"Lisa?" My mother knocks. I crumple the paper and stuff it in my pocket. I know how it got into the streetcar.

"Lisa, may I come in?"

"Yes, Mother."

She opens the door.

"Lisa," she says, "where were you?"

"Nowhere," I answer. "Just walking."

"Were you with a friend?"

"No."

"Lisa, I want you straight home or I want to know where you are. Otherwise I worry."

"Yes, Mother."

She closes the door. I throw off my jacket and plop down on my bed. One more problem I hadn't thought of. She'll want to know where I am every minute. I'll just have to start making up excuses, like going to Susanne's or something. I wait impatiently for Stefan to get home. He's always home for supper so he can listen to the radio later. I'll have to convince him to let me help.

FOUR

Waiting to Hear

"If you don't let me help," I whisper to Stefan, whom I've cornered in his room, "I'll do it by myself."

"How?" He looks at me and shakes his head, benevolent, condescending, smiling.

"How?" I say, ready for a fight. "I'll tell you how." How, I think to myself desperately. "I'll follow you, pick up one of the leaflets, make copies by hand at home, and give them out!"

I grin defiantly at him, sit back on the bed, and look as superior as I can.

The smile fades from his face. He looks at me thoughtfully. "You could get caught," he says quietly, now deadly serious. "And anyway, you wouldn't be very effective alone."

"I know I wouldn't!" I explode—in a whisper. "But you have to let me help. Look, I'm not asking you to let me go on one of your secret missions." Stefan looks at me in surprise. "Come on, I'm not blind," I add. Or deaf, I think to myself. "I just want to do what I can. People should know the truth, what's really happening. And I can help."

"I'll have to check it out first," he replies.

"They'll ask you," I say, "they'll ask you, 'Can she do it?' What'll you say?"

There's an endless pause as he looks at me. I feel my whole life rests on what he says next. You always pretend you couldn't care less what your stupid, overbearing brother thinks, but you care, all right.

"I'll say that they can trust you. And," he adds, breaking into a grin, "that you're a good runner."

I start breathing again—no wonder I was getting dizzy—and give him a big bear hug that almost knocks him over.

"I hope," he says, looking away from me, suddenly all embarrassed, "that I won't regret this."

"I won't let you down, Stefan!"

"No, I know that," he answers gently, "but I hope I'm not letting you down. Or Mother and Father. If they knew I was letting you get involved . . ."

"Don't think that way, Stefan. I want to. It's not you. I'd find some way to do it, with or without you."

"All right," he says. "Tomorrow, after supper, I'll let you know."

* * *

The next morning Erik and I arrive at school to find barbed wire all around the school yard, and thin, scrawny, dirty men in prison uniforms silently gazing at us through the wire. Erik speaks to a couple of them, but they don't answer, and you can tell that they don't understand him. Then he asks where they're from, but he can't seem to find the right language. All we know is that they're not Swedish, Norwegian, Italian, French, or German. Erik has tried all those languages. Maybe Polish. They look terrible.

All of a sudden I feel so fat and healthy. I take my lunch out of my book bag and pass the sandwich and apple through to one of the prisoners. He smiles. He has no teeth. I guess he'll have to give the apple to someone else.

A guard sees us and yells at us to get away. We hurry to the entrance of the school, where Mrs. Jensen is waiting for us.

"Everyone must go to Hellerup school," she says.

"But it's full already," I say.

"School will only be every other day from now on," she replies. "Now hurry, I'll meet you there."

I say to Erik, "Well, it's like what your dad said about the trains running on time—there are *some* good things about the Germans being here."

I was just kidding Erik, but for the first time since the invasion I can see he is genuinely upset.

"You think that's good, do you?" he says. "How can I keep my grades up without all my classes?"

I stand still, thunderstruck. "You're crazy, you know

that?" I laugh, and we hurry over to Hellerup school.

There are a million kids there, and everything is in utter chaos. I find Susanne, and we hang around together until Mrs. Jensen comes and shows us to our new room. There are already kids in it, and we have to share desks. I pick out the cutest boy in the class and memorize where he sits.

"That's my desk," I whisper to Susanne. She giggles and picks the desk behind mine. Then Mrs. Jensen sends us home for the day with a ton of homework.

I spend most of the day working and waiting for Stefan. I can hardly stand it. Finally he comes home just as we're sitting down to eat. I keep trying to catch his eye, but he acts as if nothing special is happening. The second he goes into his room after supper, I'm in after him.

"Well?" I say.

"Yes," he says. I begin to go after him to give him another bear hug, but he fights me off. "Come on, have some pity," he says.

I sit down then, all smiles.

"You volunteer to pick up the laundry," he says.

I groan. I'd rather be in a shoot-out than have to drag all those bags back from the laundry. It's at least two blocks away.

"The laundry," he repeats sternly. "Not the place we usually use, but the shop one block away, over on Praesteøgade. It's called Nansen's Laundry. You go in at exactly three P.M. You ask for Søren Sørensen's clean laundry. They will give you a bag. It will be filled with underground newspapers. You get on the first streetcar you see and start to leave piles of them behind. Get off, get on another streetcar, and so on, until your bag is empty. Then go to our laundry and pick up Mother's."

"But how will I explain being gone for so long?" I ask.

"I don't know," he says. "You figure it out."

It was just starting to sink in, what I was going to do.

"How often do I do this?"

"Once every two weeks."

"When do I start?"

"Friday."

FIVE

My First Mission

It's Friday. I'm on my way to Nansen's Laundry. I smile a little thinking of how Mother's jaw dropped when I volunteered to pick up the clean laundry. I'll be gone way longer than a trip to pick up the laundry would take, but I have an idea. There's only one problem. I'll have to lie. I started lying before, when I told her I'd been out walking—really, I was running. I'd never lied to her before, not about something important. Never mind, I tell myself, that could be the least of your worries today. And you know she'd never let you do this if she found out. Never.

I see the shop. It should be just three. I left the house at five minutes to.

I walk in the door. There's an old man behind the counter. He's got white hair and he's stooped. My stomach starts to feel funny. I have a pretty ridiculous stomach. If I get sick, I always get it in my stomach, nowhere else. The number of colds I've had I could count on my two hands, but stomachaches and upsets I couldn't count at all. And when I get nervous, like before examinations—I don't know how to put this delicately—I throw up a lot. Now I try taking deep breaths.

Lisa, you idiot, I say to myself, you can't get sick now. They'll never let you do this again.

I walk up to the counter and, in my biggest, bravest voice, ask for Søren Sørensen's laundry.

The old man looks at me with a little smile on his face. "No need to shout, young one. I'm old but not deaf. Just a minute." He goes into the back of the shop.

A much younger man comes out from the back, carrying a medium-sized laundry bag marked "S.S." I have to smile. At least they have a sense of humor. He hands it to me.

"Bring the bag back when you're all done," he tells me.

"I was wondering," I say to him, "could I tell my mother I saw a sign here saying you needed some help every once in a while? After school?"

"Can she be trusted?" he asks. "Once she knows our name . . ."

"Oh, yes," I assure him, "she can."

He nods in agreement.

Good. Now I have an alibi.

I take the bag from the counter and heave it over my shoulder. Oh, boy, is it heavy! It's soft around the outside, though; they must have padded it with real laundry. I head outside and find the closest streetcar stop. I wait. My heart is pounding. My stomach is doing major flip-flops. I feel everyone must know what I have in this bag. What if someone on the streetcar sees what I'm doing and turns me in? What if some German stops me, just to harass me, just to scare me, and looks in my bag? I try to keep breathing, long, slow breaths.

The streetcar comes. I pay, get on, find a single seat. Good, it's not terribly crowded. No one is sitting in the seats opposite me. I reach down casually into the bag. I can feel the papers. I get my hand around a large bundle and begin to draw them out. The streetcar stops for more passengers, and I look up just to check—oh, my God, two German soldiers are coming down the aisle. They sit down on the two seats right across from me. I shove the papers back in the bag and stare out the window. Stay calm. You're just a young girl carrying home the laundry.

I glance over at them. One of them is looking right at me. He whispers something to the other one. They both laugh. Now they're looking me up and down. I can't wait till they get suspicious. We must be almost at the next stop; I get up, the bag dragging behind me, the string pulled tight. Oh, no, my stomach—I think I'm going to—I've got to get off—

Suddenly the streetcar veers around a corner. I lose my balance, lunging right at the soldiers, and throw up all over them. They start to jump up. I back away toward the door, saying something. I think it's "Oh, my God." They're too stunned to do anything but curse.

Then I see one staring down at the laundry bag, and he looks up with his eyes burning—but now we're at the stop, and it's funny but about twenty people, other passengers, are suddenly standing between me and them, and someone is pushing me off the car whispering, "Go, go."

I leap off, dragging my bag, run into the grass and trees beside the stop, and finish throwing up. Then I sink down by my sack. I'm weak, I'm shaking, I think I'm crying, and my mouth tastes terrible. I want to go home. How did I get myself into this? I think back to the streetcar. All those people—they saved me. Maybe they saved my life.

Finally I try to pull myself together. I look around. Another streetcar is coming. I don't give myself time to think; I can't go back with a full bag. All those people who stopped the Germans for me, they want what I have.

I get into the car and take a seat. It's getting crowded now with school kids and people coming home from work. I reach into the laundry bag and grab a bundle of papers. I wait until just before the next stop. I leave a bundle on the floor, then get up and get off. I laugh. The people who get off with me look at me. But I did it. I did it!

I see a streetcar coming the opposite way and I run across the road and get on. I'll have to figure out a way to make some money. This could get expensive. I sit down, leave a pile, get off. Get on another streetcar. After two more trips, my bag is empty of papers. I take a streetcar back to the laundry, walk in, look at the clock. It's four-thirty. The man with the white hair smiles. I smile at him and give him the bag. He gives me ten øre.

"I forgot this," he says.

"But—" I say.

"No, no. We know you don't have any money of your own. See you in a couple of weeks."

I nod, walk out, pick up our real laundry, and go home. Mother seems to accept my explanation, although I'm sure she'll check. That's all right. They'll back me up.

After supper Stefan motions me into his room.

"How did it go?" he says, really interested.

We sit on the bed and I start to tell him. I get up to the point where I got sick. "You won't hold this against me?" I ask.

"No, no," he says. "Tell me, whatever."

I tell him.

"You did what?"

"I threw up all over them. You should have seen the look on their faces."

A slow smile spreads across his face. Then he's laughing.

"It wasn't funny!" I exclaim. "I could've been captured. If it wasn't for—"

Stefan is rolling off the bed, holding his stomach, he's laughing so hard. I think of the shocked look on the Germans' faces; how they'd have to walk around smelling until they could change their uniforms. It starts with a little giggle, but soon I'm on the floor with

Stefan. We are both screaming with laughter, tears rolling down our faces.

My mother and father peer in the door.

"I'm glad they can find something to laugh about," I hear my father say to my mother.

If only he knew. If only he knew!

SIX

My Fourteenth Birthday

It's so bright in a hospital. Who can sleep? I sit on my cot and I can't help but think back. How can a brain remember so much, so clearly? My fourteenth birthday. My God, what a day that was. How could so much all get squeezed into one little day?

It was last year—March 14, 1942. The Germans had been in Denmark for almost two years. For over a year, since that December when I first started putting newspapers on streetcars, I'd been busy. Very busy. I'd go to school two or three days a week, two days one week, three days the next. The rest of the time I'd spend doing homework—which we had a lot of since we weren't in school every day—and folding underground bulletins, putting them in envelopes, and addressing them. I'd be given lists of names for mailings and lots of stamps. I'd have to be very careful when I went to mail them. It was pretty boring work. I'd bother Stefan to let me go with him, wherever he went, but he wouldn't hear of it. He got his messages through Radio Free Denmark—I'd figured that much out. I wasn't as much of a pea brain as he thought. It was some sort of code, if only I knew what!

I still made the rounds on streetcars, and by then I was managing to keep my stomach under control. Susanne and I spent lots of time together, too. We'd sew and resew our clothes so we looked half decent. Susanne had a crush on Erik. Isn't that amazing? Erik, of all people. He was still busy pretending the war wasn't happening, and that afternoon—my birthday—I was going to pretend so, too. Susanne's parents ran a wonderful dance hall on Langelandsgade. It was called Minerva, and at night adults could go there and eat in the dining room and dance, but now they'd started to have matinees in the afternoon because of the seven P.M. curfew. They had a real band playing swing—even though the Germans hated swing because it was American. You were supposed to be fifteen, but they were going to let me come that day because it was my birthday. I remember standing in my room, looking in the mirror. . . .

Erik is going to take me. I can't wait. I'm actually wearing a new dress. It's white, made from a piece of parachute that Stefan brought home for me. And real white gloves, too, not the green ones made of fishskin everyone else is wearing. If only I hadn't grown so much in the last year. I simply can't fit into my old coat, so I have to wear one of these awful coats woven out of wood fiber and cardboard. It's brown and it itches. But the weather is typical March weather, cold and rainy, so I need something.

I think Jesper is going to come along with Stefan. I hope so. He's very cute and much more sensitive than that clod Stefan. I don't know how they can even be friends. I've done my hair in a French braid. I'm so tall I could easily pass for eighteen. And I am, well, developing rather well. No one is more shocked than I am to see it. Now if I could just stop tripping over myself and become graceful like Mother. Oh, I hope I don't make a fool of myself at the dance hall. Susanne and I have been practicing together for months. I wonder if Jesper will . . .

Who's that I hear? Father? It's only one-thirty; he shouldn't be home. Mother is here, of course, because it's Saturday, but Father had an operation at two. He sounds awfully strange.

I go to my door and open it. Father's slumped in his chair in the living room, his face in his hands. He's sobbing, and then screaming and sobbing. Mother is sitting beside him, stroking his head. They don't notice me. He's trying to tell her what happened, but the words don't seem to want to come out.

"They said . . . they said . . . they knew we were harboring criminals, resistance fighters, operating on them, hiding them in the hospital, and they said . . . they said this was just a warning . . . a *warning*. I was all gowned. I was just scrubbing. Nurse Hansen stopped me in the scrub room for a minute—she wanted to discuss a case—and that was when they burst through into the operating room. They had machine guns. They machine-gunned everyone, the patient, too. It was . . . it was a woman, a difficult birth, the baby . . . Niels, he was in there, four nurses—"

"Who? Who?" my mother asks.

"Lene Karlsen, Tove Albrechts, Hanne Gudmundsen, Ingemor Nielsen. All murdered."

"And Niels," whispers my mother.

A picture flashes through my mind of us all together on Dr. Knudsen's boat, the sun sparkling on the water, Dr. Knudsen giving Inge a big bear hug.

"The mother was killed, too, shot through the head, but I did a Caesarean, saved the baby. It's a fine baby, healthy, beautiful. The father went mad. He'd been waiting outside. He ran in, saw everything, went after them with his bare hands. They shot him casually, as if he were a dog."

My mother has opened the cupboard and poured my father a glass of schnapps. She puts it in his hands; he drinks it without noticing. He looks at her. His eyes are red, wild.

"What kind of world are we living in?" he cries.

Suddenly there is a knock at the door. It must be Erik. My mother turns and sees me. She comes over to me quickly and places a kiss on my forehead.

"You look beautiful, darling. You go ahead. I'll stay with your father."

"But I can't go now. I—"

"Yes you can," she says firmly. "It's your birthday, and no damned German is going to keep you at home, locked away. Tomorrow we'll go to see Tove and Inge. Tomorrow. Now go."

I've never heard so much hatred in her voice, like venom. I run into my room, get my purse, and am out the door. My father doesn't even see me.

"Hi!" says Erik, all bright and smiles.

"Oh, shut up," I say, and we walk in silence to the dance hall.

The Germans manage to ruin everything, even the one nice day I had planned. I keep thinking of that baby with no one to look after it, of Dr. Knudsen. Of Inge. Of how close Father came to being shot.

I've seen the dance hall lots of times, of course. Susanne and I come down here to practice dancing. Unlike me, she's just the right height, with long white-blond hair and blue eyes and, well, she's just perfect looking, really. And she's smart. She's an only child with no stupid older brothers, so I like to spend time here. We pretend and play and dance. Her parents are really nice, too—well, her father is a bit strict, but I guess with an only child he worries more. The hall is large, and it even has chandeliers. Everyone is sitting at tables. Susanne, Stefan, and Jesper are all at one table, and we join them. Everyone wishes me a happy birthday, but I can barely speak. The band is playing a waltz. And Jesper asks me to dance. I'm feeling so rotten I don't even get excited. I just nod dumbly and follow him. We start to dance. He looks me in the eye.

"What is it, Lisa?" he says. "You don't seem like a birthday girl to me."

I spill out the whole story, tears streaming down my cheeks as I talk.

"What kind of world do we live in, Jesper?" I echo Father's words. "Is it worth living at all?"

His hand grips mine tightly. His eyes look so sad. They're gray, and his brown hair is getting a little damp around his forehead. He has a nice, square, strong face, and he's actually a little taller than I am.

"Of course it's worth it, Lisa. We're young. We'll get rid of them, and then it'll be up to us to make a better world.

"Come on, now," he adds. "Your mission for this afternoon is not to let them ruin your birthday. All right?"

I manage a small smile, take a handkerchief out of my purse, and dry my face.

"Good for you."

A swing number has started. Everyone is doing the jitterbug.

"Now, let's really dance!"

Despite everything, it has probably been the most wonderful birthday of my life, I think to myself as Erik, Stefan, and I saunter home around dinnertime. I danced the whole afternoon, almost, with Jesper. I think he's absolutely perfect.

On the way home I tell Erik and Stefan about what happened at the hospital. They're both really upset—the color seems to drain from Stefan's face, while Erik gets all flushed. For a while we walk in silence.

"It's horrible," Erik mumbles.

"Oh, be quiet," Stefan snaps. "I don't want to hear any of your phony sympathy."

"It's not phony!" Erik protests. "You don't have to talk to me that way. It's not my fault."

"No," says Stefan, "it isn't your fault. But you sure aren't doing anything to change things."

"I'm staying out of trouble," says Erik firmly. "I'm just minding my own business. And if those people at the hospital had minded their own business, the Germans would've left them alone, too."

"And when they tried to burn the synagogue? I guess if the Jews had minded their own business, that wouldn't have happened either?" Stefan is talking very quietly, too quietly. His jaw is clenched; his eyes are blazing.

"We don't know that was the Germans," Erik says reasonably. "It could have just been the Danish Nazis."

"That's not the point!" Stefan explodes, as he lunges for Erik. I have to grab him and hold him back.

"Stefan!" I scream. "Stop it. Run, Erik!" Erik runs.

"Good-bye," I shout after him. "Thanks for coming today!"

He waves good-bye. "Thank you," he calls to me. And then he shouts, "Calm down, Stefan. That temper will get you in trouble someday!" He runs out of sight around the corner.

"This temper will get *him* into trouble someday," mutters Stefan, and we hurry home.

SEVEN

Sarah

For a minute I think Stefan and I are at the wrong apartment. I'm sure I can hear a baby crying. We open the door. My father is carrying the tiniest bundle I've ever seen. He is gently shaking it up and down and calling anxiously to Mother.

"Is it ready yet?"

My mother comes in with a milk bottle, takes the bundle, and sits down with it. Soon all is quiet.

Stefan and I creep over to have a look. It is a pink, wrinkled mess as far as I can see, and I'm about to say something about how revolting it looks when Stefan shocks me to death by going all mushy and tickling it.

"Is this the baby whose parents were shot?" he asks.

What an idiot I am. Why didn't I think of that? My father nods.

"It turns out," he says, "that the baby has no relatives here. The grandparents live in Frederikshavn and are too old to make the trip. There's an uncle somewhere, but we can't locate him. He may have been captured by the Germans, be in prison, we don't know. We'll keep looking, but in the meantime I felt . . ."

I throw my arms around Father and give him a big hug.

"Don't worry, Father," I say. "We'll manage, we'll all help."

"Yes," says Mother, "we'll have to. I was thinking, Lisa, that if you and Stefan can take care of the baby on your days off, I can arrange my schedule to be here when you're at school."

Then it occurs to me. I don't know whether I have a new brother or a new sister. I mentally cross my fingers and ask, "Is it a boy or a girl?"

"A girl," Father answers. "Just before I went to scrub, I talked to the mother. She told me that if it was a girl they wanted to name it Sarah, and that she was so sure it was a girl she hadn't even thought of a boy's name." His voice cracks a little as he continues. "That was the last thing she said to me."

We look down at the little wrinkled baby guzzling her milk, so happy, a little orphan. I start to cry.

I'm lying in bed, trying to sleep. I've always wanted a sister. Sarah. My sister Sarah. My very own baby sister. I wonder if she'll be able to stay with us after the war, if the war ever ends—

What was that? I sit up in bed. A huge explosion just

rocked our building. The baby starts to scream. I run out into the living room. I know I'm not allowed to open the black curtains, but I can't stop myself.

"Lisa! Get away from there!" screams my mother.

Stefan grabs me and pulls me away from the window. I run around shutting off the lights, then go to the window again. This time Stefan goes with me. There is a large fire blazing only blocks away, around where Susanne lives. Suddenly I have an awful feeling in the pit of my stomach. But I'm being silly. Hundreds of people live over there; why should anything happen to *her*? That's just dumb. Everyone else goes back to bed after a while, but I can't go to sleep. I sit in Father's big chair.

Soon I hear a light knock on the door, just a tiny knock, but it's almost as if I've been waiting for it. The feeling in my stomach gets worse. I don't want to answer. I don't want to see what's on the other side of the door. I've had enough for one day. My birthday, my fourteenth. The knock comes again. Why am I still sitting here? I have to go. I push myself out of the chair, make my way across the room, each step feeling so heavy I could be wading through water. I turn on the light. I open the door.

Susanne is looking at me. She has no hair—only a charred frizz is left. Her clothes are simply tatters. She is covered in blisters. I look at her. I think I'm screaming. I must be. Someone—Stefan?—has a hand over my mouth. Father is carrying Susanne in to my bed. Stefan is slapping my face. Why is he doing that? It hurts. But I stop screaming.

I'm looking at Susanne. She doesn't see me. She's moaning softly. Father is giving her a needle. She falls . . . asleep? unconscious?

"I must get her to the hospital," Father says. "Call Lars. Get an ambulance here." He wraps Susanne loosely in a clean sheet to keep her warm. We hear the siren.

"Can I go?" I ask.

"No," he says. Then he and Stefan carry her downstairs.

"They played swing at the dance hall," my mother says numbly, trying to comfort the wailing baby.

"What?" I say, not understanding.

"They played swing. The Germans couldn't stand that so they blew up the dance hall. I'm sure that's what happened. They just blew it up."

"But what about her parents?" I ask.

"We'll know tomorrow."

I wait up all night for Stefan and Father. Finally the doorknob turns. It's Stefan.

He looks at me.

"She'll live," he says. "The burns aren't serious." He takes my hands. "Lisa, I'm sorry, but her parents—they're both dead."

I can't cry. Why can't I cry? I cried for Sarah's parents, and I didn't even know them. Why can't I cry now? I'm so tired. I get into bed and sleep. And sleep.

EIGHT

Susanne

"Where do you think you're going?" I whisper, grabbing Susanne by the arm. She's been living with us for months now, eating, sleeping, going to school, helping with Sarah. Everything is normal, except for one thing: Susanne won't talk. She won't cry, either, or smile. The burns healed well; she has no scars, and she looks as beautiful as ever. But so solemn—her eyes always look dull and heavy, as if she's about to fall asleep. Father says she just needs time. But now—what is she doing now? Really losing her mind? I say something to that effect, but she doesn't answer. She just shakes me off and slips out the door. Father's out, Mother is in the kitchen with Sarah, and Stefan has just left. Susanne runs out without even a sweater. It's August, but it's getting cool at night. I can't let her go alone. I run after her.

Susanne pulls her bike out of the foyer and into the street. I grab mine and follow her. Once outside, I see that Stefan is already on his bike, riding down the street. She leaps onto hers and starts to follow him. She's doing something I've always wanted to do but never dared. I know what he does these nights he goes out. Well, I don't know what exactly, but I'd love to know.

Now, though, I'm pretty scared. I mean, dreaming about going with him and actually going are two very different things. It's dark. And if the Germans catch us, two young girls—well, they've started going really wild this summer. Whenever the resistance bombs a factory or blows up a rail line or kills an informer, they gather up any Danes they can find and shoot them—just like that. And for each German soldier killed, they shoot five of us. I have no choice. I follow her.

Stefan has stopped in front of a house, parked his bike, and got into a car. Good. Susanne will have to give up. I put on some speed and catch up to her.

"Susanne," I hiss, "let's go home! My brother will kill us."

Susanne looks at me. Then—she speaks!

"You go, Lisa. I can't."

I'm so stunned I can't respond. The car is moving and Susanne is following it, going as fast as she can. I have no choice. I follow, too.

They are heading for the outskirts of town, driving slowly. Sweat is pouring off me, and the night air is chilling me. I'm using all my strength. How can Susanne keep it up?

The car stops. The men get out and Susanne rides straight up to them. With me behind her. Oh, Stefan's going to kill me! The men are standing still. They are silent. There are two others plus Stefan, the others much older. They are all pointing their guns straight at us.

"I have to help," Susanne says firmly, walking up to them. I stagger behind her, my legs wobbly.

Stefan lowers his gun. He whispers quickly to the two others. They nod.

"Wait here," says the plump, middle-aged one. The other man is tall and lanky.

Susanne opens her mouth to object.

"You'll help," he says. "Just wait your turn."

She stands quietly.

Stefan glares at me.

I shrug.

"Keep a lookout," he snaps.

We're in an industrial area. I see them head for one of the larger buildings to our right. I know there must be guards around.

Susanne and I stay put and wait. Within five minutes, the three of them return and start unloading something from the back of the car.

"The guards are tied up in a corner of the yard," says Stefan. "Careful with this stuff." He hands us each a bottle of kerosene. "It has to be poured very carefully, in lines, until it reaches the explosives." I try not to let my hands shake.

We enter the factory. It's filled with radio components. Stefan says they're used to make V-2 bombs. He shows where the men have placed the explosives and gives us each a flashlight. It's too hard to pour the kerosene while holding the flashlight. I keep splashing. Soon Susanne and I decide to work together. I hold the light. Susanne pours. I'd spill it all over the place anyway. We make lines of kerosene from the door to the center beams where the explosives are. We finally finish.

"Put your bicycles in the car," Stefan says. "This stuff goes up pretty fast. We'll have almost no time to escape."

"But," I object, "the car won't go fast enough to—"

"This car's not a wood-burner," Stefan reassures me. "It's got real gas."

Susanne and I run outside, put our bicycles on the backseat, and climb in on top of them. Stefan and the two others stay behind to light the kerosene. They race out of the building and leap into the car. We take off, the plump, middle-aged man driving. We're only two blocks away when a huge explosion shakes the ground. Susanne starts to smile. It's the first time I've seen her smile since that night.

She whispers to me, "That was for Mama and Papa. But it was only the first." She's actually enjoying herself.

A chill runs down my spine. My God, I think, these Germans are dragging us all down to their level. How will we keep ourselves better than them?

"See this?" Stefan, who is in the front seat, turns to

us. He is holding a mean-looking object in his hand. It's two long iron nails twisted around each other so that the four prongs stick out in different directions. He opens the window and drops it on the road. He reaches to the floor, picks up more of them, and continues to drop them as we drive. "That should slow the Germans down a bit."

The driver is trying not to go too fast. He doesn't want to attract attention.

"You girls did well," the driver says, "but don't *ever* follow us like that again."

Finally they drop us a little way from home, and we untangle ourselves from our bicycles. Stefan sticks his head through the car window and talks quietly with the other man, the lanky one, but I can't hear him. As Stefan starts to leave, the man adds, "Do you want us to pick up your bike?"

"No, thanks," says Stefan. "I'll get it tomorrow when we meet."

The strangest thing about the whole evening is that when we walk in, Mother looks at us, pauses, and then says quite casually, "Did you have a good evening?"

"Very good," replies Susanne.

Mother smiles and says, "Good. I hope you were careful."

Stefan starts to say something, then stops himself, but he follows us into our room. We've been sharing my room since—well, since Susanne's been here.

Stefan shuts the door. I wonder if he'll actually hit me this time.

"Are you two out of your minds?" he shouts.

"I had to do it," Susanne says. "I have to help you." She is hard, like steel.

Stefan looks at her. I think, with all the tension and excitement, it's just now occurred to him that she's begun talking again. He actually smiles at her.

"Susanne," he says, then pauses and looks at her. "All right, I'll see if I can get permission to bring you along—get you involved."

"Thank you, Stefan," she says, and she's smiling again. I can hardly believe it.

NINE

Guns and Secrets

It's our day off school, and I've been stuffing envelopes all morning. There's a warm summer breeze blowing in through my window. It's such a relief to be working in just a skirt and blouse. In the winter I had to sit in my coat and stuff envelopes with gloves on. Gas is rationed, so we could only heat one room, the living room, and it was horribly cold in the bedrooms.

I have to be extra careful these days. Every time I'm given a list of names and addresses, I burn it right after I've used it. If the Germans got hold of it, it would be a complete disaster. And they're really cracking down now. The whole country seems to have woken up—finally. There are street demonstrations against the Germans all the time, and at least six or seven resistance bombings a day, and the Germans are going crazy.

They're bringing out more troops and making more arrests, but that just gets everyone madder, so there are more riots and demonstrations.

I hope Susanne hasn't been caught in some mob. I wonder where she is. She left after breakfast—no explanation, just ran off.

Sarah is sleeping. She's a beautiful baby, with big brown eyes and silky brown hair and a round face, all cheeks. She's been with us a year and a half now—my fifteenth birthday came and went without any more new relatives—and I couldn't love her more if she were my own sister. She talks already. She makes little sentences like "Go sleep," "Go bye," "I hungry," stuff like that.

Erik is supposed to drop over this afternoon. Susanne quickly got over her crush on him. She doesn't have time for that sort of thing. But he developed a massive crush on her and is always hanging around now. It drives her crazy. I don't have crushes—I'm much too old for that kind of nonsense. I only wish I could stop holding my breath every time Stefan comes home because I'm hoping Jesper will be with him. It makes me feel really stupid. Jesper took me out for my fifteenth birthday. Stefan told me he tried to talk some sense into him. Why do brothers have to make a point of being awful?

Jesper took me to Tivoli. It was a wonderful day. He told me he'd been at Victor Borge's last performance there. He said the front rows were filled with German soldiers. Borge walked onto the stage goose-stepping and sticking his arm out in the Nazi salute. All the Germans leaped up and saluted back. Then he turned to the audience and said, "Has anybody seen my dog? He's about *so* high," using his arm to show that that's what he'd meant all along. Well, the Germans were so mad! The audience roared with laughter and applause. The Germans went after him, but somehow people smuggled him out the back of the theater. He's in the United States now. Oh, I laughed so hard my sides hurt. Jesper described it so perfectly I felt I'd been there myself. We ate and went on rides and played some of the games. And I tried hard not to see the Germans all around us. . . .

The door slams and Susanne runs into our room. Her face is flushed. She pulls a gun out of her purse.

"We've got to hide this," she says.

I jump up and slam our door shut. "What have you been doing?" I ask.

"Remember those two men we met when we followed Stefan?" she asks, still panting and now shaking a little.

I nod.

"They're both dead."

"How?" I ask. "What happened?"

"They were informed on by a new member of the group. We were suspicious of him, and I've been watching his house—Stefan and I—and yesterday we saw him meet a Gestapo officer. I was the one who did it. I insisted on doing it. Stefan and Jesper are taking him for a little boat trip now, his one-way ticket to Sweden."

Now I know what she's talking about. She's shot him,

and the boys are dumping his body into the sea. That way the Germans can't be sure we've killed him, and they may not retaliate so quickly.

I can't find anything to say. She's shot him. Suddenly I'm far more worried about something else.

"Did he know about Stefan?" I ask.

"No, those two were his only contacts."

I sigh with relief, unable to speak for a moment, my mouth is so dry. I can see them so clearly, bursting in here, dragging Stefan away. . . . Thank goodness the resistance keep their groups, cells, to three or four people. Each cell has only one contact person to another cell, so if there's an informer—or what's more likely, if someone cracks under torture—he can't betray so many people.

"What shall we do with this?" she asks. The gun—I'd almost forgotten it.

I have an idea. There's a loose floorboard in my closet that no one has had time to fix. I pry it up. Now I really have a shock. There are already six guns and a submachine gun down there. I gasp.

Susanne comes and looks over my shoulder.

"Stefan?" she says.

"Who knows?" I say, feeling like giggling. "It could even be Mother. You never know with this family."

She grins and adds her gun to the collection.

Susanne has just killed a man. Shot him in cold blood. Could I do the same? I think back to the mission she and I were on last week, with Stefan and an older man, Olaf. We blew up a shoe factory. About ten blocks from the blast, a German patrol car stopped us. I was riding in the front seat with Olaf. The officers came up to our car, one on each side, shoving their guns against Olaf's head and mine. Oh, thank God for my stomach. I immediately threw up on the car floor.

"We're taking her to the hospital," said Olaf in broken German. "She has a terrible stomach pain. We think it's her appendix." I moaned and groaned and clutched my stomach. I could feel the gun in my hand, hidden by my sweater. If they ordered us out of the car, I'd have to use it. I'd have to shoot the German soldier right through the head. I looked up at his face. He was around forty, big and tough. I looked at the other one. He looked so young! Maybe Stefan's age. I could see Olaf holding his gun ready under his jacket. They looked at each other, the soldiers. Could I do it? Could I shoot him? The one nearest me wrinkled his nose at the smell. I moaned again.

"Go on," he said.

Olaf drove off. His poor car . . .

Someone is pounding on the apartment door. My heart stops. Quickly we replace the floorboard and go to the door.

"It's me, Erik!" the voice says. "Let me in!"

We open the door. The baby starts to cry, and I run for her.

"The Germans are taking over!" Erik says, and I realize there is gunfire in the distance.

Susanne laughs. "You're just a few years late, Erik," she says scornfully.

"No, they've declared martial law," he says. "They're arresting the police, taking over our army. Parliament is dissolved. The chief rabbi has been arrested, too. Rabbi Melchior is taking his place." As he speaks, there's a burst of explosions coming from the direction of the harbor. "That's our navy," he says. "We're sinking our own ships rather than let the Germans have them."

I see that Erik is really upset. "I was walking here, and they started firing at people for nothing," he says. "There was this little kid—I don't know, maybe ten—"

"Still think you should just mind your own business?" asks Susanne sharply.

He looks up and I can see tears in his eyes. She's hit him where it hurts.

"Well, maybe—maybe if there hadn't been so much sabotage, if we'd cooperated . . ."

"*Ooooh!*" Susanne screams. "You're hopeless, hopeless! Don't you understand, Erik? They're bullies! And the only thing a bully understands is someone standing up to him and saying, 'We're not afraid of you, and we're not going to let you walk all over us!'"

Erik shakes his head. He's all mixed up, and I don't blame him. He believes in peace, and it's not getting him anywhere. I look at Susanne. She's my best friend. She just killed a man, and she doesn't feel any remorse. But I feel it for her. For all of us.

"Look what's happening to us," I murmur to myself.

Susanne looks at me, and for a moment I know she understands. Then her eyes get hard. "We don't have time for sentiment. We have to do what we have to do. You'd better not go out, Erik."

Erik agrees. He stays with us. It's very late before Mother and Stefan finally get home. Father doesn't come home all night. I imagine he has a lot of work at the hospital today. Too much. Way too much.

TEN

Am I So Different?

"It's not safe at all anymore," says Mother. "I don't even want to take Sarah out for a walk."

The Schalburg Corps, our very own Danish traitors, our own Nazi regiment, is running wild now. They're looting, burning, shooting at will. . . . I asked Mother how one Dane could betray another Dane like that. She said some people will do anything to feel powerful and superior.

We're all sitting around the table, eating. Father looks very thin and worn. He's been working almost nonstop for a month now, since August, when martial law was declared. There's been another shooting at the hospital. More of his friends and colleagues killed.

"Susanne," he says suddenly, coming out of his reverie, "you're going to have to leave Copenhagen tomorrow."

"What!" we both exclaim together.

"Tomorrow," he says firmly. "The other night the Nazis broke into the Jewish Community Center and stole a list of all the names. Today a special detail of Eichmann's goons has arrived in Copenhagen."

"No, Father, it can't be!" I cry. I'm not willing to accept what he's getting at. What does it matter that we are Jewish? I don't feel any different from anyone else, and I'm not treated differently. Now will I have to be only a Jew? Is being a Jew all that's important about me? The very name Eichmann makes me feel sick to my stomach.

Erik's father said maybe the trains would run on time with the Germans here. Well, Eichmann will make sure of that. It's his speciality. We know all about Eichmann and his trainloads full of Jews. The trains that run like clockwork. Never missing a delivery to the concentration camps. We know what happens in the camps, too. We hear it on Radio Free Denmark. I read it in the newspapers that I put on the streetcars.

Father looks at me. He's tired.

"Lisa," he says. I can see he's almost too tired to talk, but he makes an effort. "Lisa, perhaps it won't happen here. But we know what has happened in every other occupied country. The Jews are rounded up and sent to concentration camps. And we know what happens to them there. They are killed. It's that simple. When I think of all the children . . ." He looks at Sarah, nestled in Mother's arms. "If there were someone I could give her to, I would," he says. "Why should she suffer because we're Jewish?"

Susanne's face is white. She looks like a little girl now, little and scared.

"But you're my family," she whispers. "Where can I go?"

"I've called your aunt and uncle in Aarhus," says Father. "They've got four young children. You can help them. They're expecting you."

"They didn't want me before," she says bitterly. "Why now?"

"Well," says Father, "you were younger then, and they already had four children under six. Your aunt just didn't know how she'd manage. And remember, you weren't talking. She couldn't have cared for you properly. Besides, we wanted you."

"And now I'm to be her private baby-sitter," snorts Susanne.

"Susanne," Father says quietly, "we love you. But you aren't Jewish. Why should you suffer, perhaps die, needlessly?" He winks at her. "Maybe you'll find other things to do in Aarhus." It's just a tiny wink, but I catch it and so does she, and she can't help but smile a bit.

She is wavering. "I don't know," she says, looking at me.

I know she doesn't want to desert me.

"I want you to be safe," I say. "If anything happened to you, I'd blame myself. You'd be in trouble just because we're friends."

"That's a good reason to be in trouble," Susanne argues.

I can't stand it. I'm scared. Are we going to be hunted down like rats? Is it true they have gas chambers where Jews are stripped, then put into huge showers and gassed to death? I feel sick.

"I don't want your death on my conscience!" I blurt out. "I'm going to have enough to worry about."

Susanne looks at my father. "I'll go," she says.

That night, in bed, Susanne and I snuggle close to each other.

"As soon as the war's over, we'll be sisters again," I say.

"If we survive," she murmurs. She pauses. "Are you ever afraid to die, Lisa?"

"Are you joking?" I sigh. "All the time. Even when I'm sitting here stuffing envelopes, I'm always listening for boots on the stairs or pounding on the door. But—I'd rather be killed than captured and tortured."

Susanne is silent for a minute. Then she says, "Remember when we used to practice dancing at my parents' dance hall, and we'd imagine being fifteen and going out with boys—"

"And you had a crush on Erik," I tease her.

"And we thought we'd go on dates together, skating in winter, swimming parties in the summer, and lots of movies, and our parents would yell at us for staying out too late. . . ."

Susanne is making a funny gulping sound. I touch

her face with my hand; it's too dark to see anything. Her cheeks are wet with tears. I put my arms around her and she sobs as if her heart is breaking.

Finally she wipes her face on the bedsheet and says, her voice fierce, "If it looks as though anything is going to happen to the Jewish people, I'm going to help them escape. You'll see. I won't just sit around in Aarhus looking after babies."

"But be careful," I whisper, squeezing her hand.

"And you," she says, "try not to trip all over yourself on your way out of the country."

"I'll try," I reply, shocked at the idea, realizing I hadn't let myself think that far. I force myself to imagine having to leave my own country.

I don't have to imagine it for long.

ELEVEN

Rosh Hashanah

Tonight is the first night of Rosh Hashanah. A new year—what will it bring? I hardly dare to think. I'm making a pastry for the special supper tonight. I have to leave in a few minutes. I got up early to do this, and now it's ready, but I still have to tell Stefan how to cook it. He's staying home with Sarah today. I have school.

I'm looking forward to going to the synagogue tonight. I like to sit beside Mother; we whisper to each other. I ask her questions, and she always has interesting answers. I like to let my mind wander, to think about life. And on Rosh Hashanah I'm always full of resolve, full of ways to improve myself.

The phone is ringing. The phone never rings. I wonder what could be so important.

I answer. "Hello?"

"Lisa?" It's Father.

"Yes, Father?"

"Lisa, I need you to come to the hospital right away. Has Mother left yet?"

"Yes."

"Then you bring Sarah to the hospital and tell Stefan to go and fetch your mother."

"But—" I begin.

"I have some urgent paperwork, and I need all the help I can get. You must come. Do you understand?"

I wasn't sure I did.

"I'm afraid there will be no service tonight at the synagogue," Father continues. "Rabbi Melchior told everyone at the early service that he'll be closing the synagogue. He's going on holiday."

I almost laugh. The rabbi going on holiday on Rosh Hashanah?

Then it hits me.

"He feels everyone should go on holiday," my father says.

All of a sudden my mouth is so dry I can barely answer him. "Yes, Father," I reply.

"Oh, and Lisa?"

"Yes?"

"You and Stefan can bring as many friends as possible to help. All right? Try to tell your friends."

"Yes, I will."

"Good-bye, Lisa."

"Good-bye, Father."

"Who was that?" Stefan calls from the bathroom, where he is changing Sarah.

I walk into the bathroom and look at Stefan.

"Father wants us at the hospital. I'm to take Sarah, and you're to go and fetch Mother."

It takes a second, then Stefan looks at me.

"It'll be all right, Lisa. Really. We'll be fine. We're used to fighting. We'll be fine."

"He says we should bring our friends. He wants us to tell people. Rabbi Melchior has closed the synagogue."

"All right," says Stefan. "I'll finish changing Sarah. You get on your bike, and go and tell anyone you can think of. When you get back, I'll get Mother and you can take Sarah to the hospital."

"All right."

"Be careful," Stefan warns as I turn to go.

"I will," I call back.

I run downstairs and pull my bicycle out of the foyer.

Who do I tell first?

Erik.

I start to ride as fast as I can. I see my friends Inge and Ebba hurrying to school.

"Inge!"

"Hi, Lisa. You're going the wrong way."

"I'm going to Erik's. Inge, you have to tell Tove and Lone that the Germans are planning to round up all the Jews tonight. Everyone must go into hiding. Tell them to leave school and go find their parents."

"Oh no, Lisa, it's not true," Inge protests.

"Of course it's true!" I yell. "Just tell them."

They look as if I've hit them.

Ebba says, "We'll tell them. And anyone else we can find."

"Good," I say. "Thanks."

"Will you be all right, Lisa?" asks Ebba.

"I'll be fine."

I wave good-bye and hurry over to Erik's. I jump off my bicycle and race into his apartment house. He lives in an apartment on the first floor. I pound on the door.

The door is opened cautiously. It's his mother.

"Hello, Cousin Anne," I say. "May I come in?"

"Yes, of course, Lisa," she says. "How nice to see you. But you shouldn't pound so on the door, dear. It frightened me. I thought only the Germans pounded like that."

"I'm sorry," I say, not quite paying attention. "Where's Erik? Has he left for school already?"

"Why, he's gone to see his grandparents in Roskilde. He'll stay with them for Rosh Hashanah. Cousin Adam and I will join them later today."

"Do they have a phone?" I ask, almost knowing the answer.

"No, dear. Why? Can't it wait?"

"No, Anne, it can't." I sit down on a chair in the living room. "My father just called from the hospital. He didn't want to say much on the phone, but it seems Rabbi Melchior announced at the morning service that the Germans are going to begin rounding us up. He's closed the synagogue."

She sinks into the chair opposite me. "No," she whispers. "No, they wouldn't."

"I think they will," I say firmly.

She starts to shake her head slowly back and forth. "It's terrible, it's terrible. They'll come and drag us away like dogs to be drowned."

"I think they're nicer to animals," I reply.

"Adam won't believe it," she says, her voice trembling. "He won't believe it." She begins to cry.

"Anne," I tell her, "you have to convince him. You can both go to Father's hospital and hide there. Then we'll all find a way to get out of the country."

"He won't go," she cries, "he won't. And how can I leave him all alone?"

"But Anne," I plead, "you must make him go. And if he really won't, then you have to go alone. You'll be of no help to him here. They won't keep you together anyway. And then he'll know that because of him, they got you too. And what about Erik?"

"Yes, Erik," she says, drying her eyes. "You must go and fetch him. He'll help me convince his father. Maybe Adam will listen to Erik." She jumps up and runs into the kitchen. She puts fifty øre into my hand.

"If you hurry, you can just catch the ten o'clock train. You'll be there by eleven. You remember the house?"

"Yes," I say, "I think so."

"And be sure to warn your cousins Hanne and Karl as well. Bring them back with you, or help them find somewhere to go. But you must leave at once."

"But Stefan's waiting for me," I protest. "He has to go and get Mother and then warn his friends."

"I'll go to your house right now, Lisa. I'll look after

Sarah until you get back. And while I wait, I can make some phone calls, tell our friends. All right?"

I nod my head. Poor Anne. She's barely gone out of the house since the Germans arrived. I know that's why she's having me go for Erik. To go herself would simply be too much for her. She quakes and trembles at the very thought of a German soldier, never mind the actual sight of one.

I pocket the money. "Will you go right away?" I ask.

"Yes. In fact, I'll leave the house with you."

She fetches her coat and we leave together, she for my house, I for the station. I wave as I ride off on my bicycle.

It's already nine-forty. I ride through town very fast. Twice I see people I know, friends of my parents, and both times I stop and tell them the news. I haven't time to try to convince them. I just hope they'll believe me.

I get to the station, park my bicycle in the rack outside, and line up in the foyer to buy my ticket. Then I hurry into the great hall. The old wooden station is packed with people, mostly soldiers. The windows on the roof admit a dim light, made dimmer still by all the smoke. I force myself not to run. I walk quickly through the haze to the far side of the hall, down the stairs to the platform, and board the train immediately.

The compartment holds six people. There are an elderly couple, a young man, and a middle-aged couple. The two couples look as though they are traveling together. They also look Jewish; I can't be sure, but the younger couple both have black curly hair. Probably they are traveling to the town where their children live, to spend Rosh Hashanah with them.

I look at the young man. He seems innocent enough, but how can you tell by looking at someone if he's to be trusted or not? You can't even tell by talking. After all, if he is a Danish Nazi, he'd pretend to hate them, just so he won't be found out. If he's a resistance fighter, he might even pretend to be a German sympathizer, or at least neutral, so no one will suspect him. It used to be that everyone would talk freely—to their neighbors, on a train, at school. Now everyone suspects everyone.

How can I warn these people without endangering us all?

The couples are chatting among themselves about spending Rosh Hashanah with their children and grandchildren. Now I know for sure that they're Jewish.

Suddenly I get an idea. It's a natural for me. I put my head between my knees and start to moan a bit.

Immediately, both women are huddled around me.

"What is it, my dear? Are you ill?"

"I feel awful," I say. "Could . . . would one of you take me to the washroom?"

"Yes, yes, of course, dear," says the older woman.

"No, Mother, you stay here," the daughter insists. "I'll take her."

She puts her arm under mine and leads me out of the compartment. The washroom is down at the end of the corridor. I stop her halfway there. There's no one around, so I try to talk quickly, before someone happens along.

"I'm all right, really, but I had to talk to you."

Her eyebrows rise.

"I didn't know if I could talk safely in front of that young man."

Again she says nothing, but nods and listens.

"Rabbi Melchior announced at services this morning that the Germans will start rounding up the Jews on Rosh Hashanah. I suppose that means tonight or tomorrow. You must warn your family and find somewhere to hide."

Now it is she who looks faint. I put a hand under her elbow.

"Are you all right?"

She nods. "Yes. Yes. I've been waiting for this. We heard about the list of names being stolen from the Community Center. But where can we go?"

"Where do your children live?"

"In Holbæk."

"Well, they must have many friends who aren't Jewish."

"Of course," she replies.

"Then I'm sure you won't have a problem. Their friends will hide you. But then you must try to get a boat to Sweden."

She takes my hand. "Thank you, young lady," she says. "What is your name?"

"Lisa."

"Lisa. My name is Jytte. Thank you, my dear. You may have saved our lives, although hiding, trying to sneak over to Sweden, all seems so impossible. I don't know. Perhaps it would be easier just to wait for the Germans. My parents aren't strong anymore."

"No, no, you mustn't," I insist. "People will help, you'll see. You have to be strong—for your parents' sake, too. You have to try. At least you'll have a fighting chance."

She shakes her head, squeezes my hand, then we go back into the compartment. The others are full of concern for my health. Soon, however, they begin to focus on Jytte.

"Why, Jytte," says her mother, "I think you've caught whatever this young lady has. You're all white."

"No," she says, "I don't think it's something you can catch. It's something you're born with."

They all give her puzzled looks. I sneak a glance at the young man, but he is peering out the window, seemingly uninterested.

And soon the train pulls into Roskilde. We say our good-byes, and I get off to find Erik.

TWELVE

Erik

In no time I find myself knocking at Erik's grandparents' front door.

Erik opens it. Needless to say, he's stunned to see me.

"Lisa! What?"

"Are you going to just stand there blabbering or are you going to ask me in?"

"Yes, well, come in," he says, backing into the house, eyeing me suspiciously. "What are you doing here?"

"Are your grandparents home?"

"Yes," he says.

"Good. I want to talk to all of you." He ushers me into the living room, where his grandfather is sitting reading. He goes to the kitchen for his grandmother.

Wonderful smells are drifting into the living room from the kitchen.

"Who's that?" asks Karl, Erik's grandfather. Karl is my grandfather's first cousin, so we are cousins, too. His eyesight is pretty bad and so is his memory. He's a tiny man, gray all over. Hanne is the opposite. She sees and remembers everything, and she's big and rosy.

"Of course, it's Lisa, Karl," says Hanne, bustling into the room. She grabs my cheek and pinches it as hard as she can between her thumb and index finger.

"Oooh, just look at her! What a beauty. Big and healthy, like an ox! Don't you remember, Karl, the last time she was here, she broke our best plate? A little clumsy, but a good child!"

She pushes me into a chair. "You sit there. I'll go get some food for you. That long trip, you must be famished."

"Hanne, Hanne, wait!" I cry. "I have to talk to you. It's very serious. Anne sent me. Come, sit down."

Hanne sits down reluctantly—rather, she perches her big frame on the edge of a chair. Erik stands.

"The Germans are going to start rounding up all the Jews," I say, not knowing how to say it in a nicer way. "Tonight. Erik is to come back to Copenhagen with me. And I'm to find you both a place to stay or else bring you, too. You can't be home tonight."

"But my cooking," wails Hanne. "I can't leave it, I've been cooking for weeks. And the kitchen is a shambles. I can't just walk out now and let the Germans find all those dirty dishes. What will they think?"

"Hanne," I say gently, "have you any friends you could stay with?"

She thinks for a moment. "Well, there's Ilse. We went to school together, you know. And we still see each other twice a week for cards."

"Then you must go over there right now and ask her."

"But," Hanne protests again, "I can't just leave everything. Who knows what those barbarians will do if they get in here?"

"Hanne," I say, "don't you think Ilse would be delighted if you took the food to her house? What a treat for her!"

"Oh," says Hanne, thinking for a moment, "well, yes, I suppose, yes, all right." She takes off her apron and goes to the front closet for her coat. "Ilse just lives one block over. I'll go and talk to her. I'll be right back."

I shake my head and, despite everything, smile a little to myself. She's not scared of the Germans; she's only worried about her kitchen and her cooking. Then I realize that Erik has been unusually silent. I look at him. He has that stubborn expression on his face. I brace myself.

"Erik, the next train is at twelve. We have to be on it. Don't you think you'd better go and pack?"

"Lisa, spare me your dramatics. Perhaps the old ones will fall for it, but not me. You're all making fools of yourselves, indulging in hysteria. Besides," he hisses, his voice low so Karl won't hear him, "I'm not even Jewish anymore."

I almost laugh. "Oh, come on, Erik, do you think

they're going to let a little thing like conversion stop them? It's your blood, your *blood*, the Nazis hate. Now go and get packed or you'll end up in a concentration camp, and I'll never see your stupid face again."

He continues to look stubborn, and he won't move.

Then I don't know what comes over me, but I hit him. I slap him really hard across the face. Twice.

He staggers back, his hand to his cheek.

"Lisa," cries Karl, "what are you doing?"

"I'm trying to knock some sense into him," I shout, tears stinging my eyes. "Do you think I like this? Do you think I like believing that anyone could do this to somebody else? But I do believe it, and I don't want those bastards to get you or him. Do you understand, Erik?" I scream. "You can't bury your head any longer. Not unless you're willing to die for it."

Karl may be old, but he understands what's happening. "Go pack," he says quietly to Erik. "Pack and go home with Lisa."

"Grandpa, if you believe Lisa, don't you want me to stay here and help you and Grandma?"

"We have friends," he says calmly. "We'll be fine. You go home and take care of your parents. Your mother wants you because your father is not going to budge. Like you, he doesn't believe they'll come for him or for any of us. You have to help get him out. You have to make him go, Erik."

Erik nods, then goes over to his grandfather and gives him a kiss. "All right, Grandpa. I'll do as you say. I think it's a big waste of time, but if it makes you feel better . . ."

"You're a good boy, Erik. You go take care of your parents."

"Yes, Grandpa."

I sit down as Erik goes to pack.

"Will you be all right, Karl?" I ask. I see his eyes are watery.

"Yes, yes. It's hard, though, at our age, having to run like frightened rabbits." He dabs at his eyes with his handkerchief.

"I know," I say. "It's even hard at my age."

We sit in silence then, until Erik comes back, his bag packed, ready to go.

The door opens and Hanne bustles back in. "It's fine, it's fine, we'll go to Ilse's. She's sending her son over to help carry the food and our luggage. I'm taking all my valuables. I won't leave anything here for them."

"We have to go, Hanne," I say.

Erik is all ready. She goes over to him and gives him a big hug. "God be with you, sweetheart," she says. "You take care of your father and mother for me."

"I will, Grandmother." He gives her a kiss on the cheek. "Please be careful."

"Don't you worry about us. We have so many friends here. They won't let anything happen to us."

Erik calls good-bye again to Karl, I give them each a kiss, and we leave.

"They'll be fine, Erik," I say. "It's you and your parents I'm worried about. Your father probably won't listen, just like you, and I don't think your mother will leave him."

We hurry to the station and get there just in time to

catch the twelve o'clock train to Copenhagen. We find an empty compartment and settle in. But as the train starts, three German soldiers and one Gestapo officer enter our compartment and sit down beside us. Wonderful, I say to myself. Perfect. They are talking rapidly and are obviously upset.

I've taken German at school, of course, and I understand it pretty well. From what I can gather, a friend of theirs shot a Dane he didn't like the looks of. A crowd—or mob, as they say—gathered, disarmed him, then beat him to death. They're swearing revenge, cursing the stupid Danes.

I begin to be afraid that soon they'll start taking out their frustration on Erik and me. I signal with my eyes that we must get out. Together we get up and try to slip past them. The one nearest the door grabs at me, laughing, but I shake him off and we run into the corridor and hurry down to the next car. We can still hear their laughter—at us, at our fear. We find an empty compartment and continue in silence, on to Copenhagen.

THIRTEEN

At the Hospital

Both Erik and I ride my bicycle. I pedal and he sits. People chuckle as they see us, but I'm so big he'd never be able to drive me.

As we park the bike in the foyer of my apartment, I wonder if everything is still all right or if the Germans could have already begun their raids. I tell myself that they'll stick to their plan and wait until the New Year starts, tonight.

We run up the stairs and enter my apartment. Everything is fine. Anne is playing on the floor with Sarah. She straightens up and gives both Erik and me a big hug.

"You have to go get your father at the shipyard, darling," she says to Erik. "I'll go home and wait for you."

"I must get down to the hospital," I say. "Father's waiting for me. Where's Stefan?"

"He went for your mother," says Anne. "Thank you for bringing Erik, dear," she calls over her shoulder as she and Erik hurry out.

"Take care," I call after them and I turn to Sarah. "Come on, Sarahle," I say, "you and I have to get ready."

I go and gather some clothes for Sarah, myself, Mother, Father, and Stefan. Just one change each, and Sarah's bottles and diapers. I pack them all in a laundry bag. Then I get the phone book.

I start to call every Jewish family I know. I tell them that the rabbi is going on holiday and that they should consider a holiday, too. As soon as possible. They understand. Then I start to look in the book for Jewish-sounding names and to call them.

I call for a couple of hours. It's three o'clock by now. I give Sarah some rye bread and a little cold fish. She's been playing with her blocks, so good, as if she knows I need her help. I dress her in a warm sweater and pants and a jacket. It's September 30 and turning chilly and damp. I hoist her up on my hip with one arm and throw the laundry bag over my other shoulder. I take a last look around. Will I ever see my home again?

I think of Susanne's words. I miss her so much. But this is no time for sentiment. I open the door and leave any pretense of normalcy behind me. Sarah and I head for the streetcar and the hospital.

Father has an office on the second floor. I knock on the door. "Come in," he calls.

I walk in. His desk is hidden under a mass of papers. He peers at me over the mess.

Suddenly a bizarre thought strikes me. What if the rabbi really *was* going on vacation, and Father really *did* need help with some paperwork, and the roundup was all in my imagination?

"Father," I say, "you didn't just need me to help with paperwork, did you?"

He looks up at me, distraught. "Where's your mother?" he asks.

"Stefan's gone for her."

"No, Lisa," he says, shaking his head sadly, "although I would like you to help me with this. I want everything in order. Once we leave, it may be a long time before we're back."

"But where can we go? Where?" I'm afraid my voice has a distinct whine to it. But if you can't whine at your own father, who can you whine at?

"Sweden, Lisa."

I know that, of course, but it's reassuring to hear him say it.

"Can I put Sarah somewhere for her nap, Father?" She's almost asleep.

"Just put a blanket down over there," he says, pointing to a corner, "then come help me here." I take her favorite blanket out of the laundry bag and place it on the floor for her. I give her her small doll made out of a blue stocking. It has white yarn for hair and white buttons for its nose and eyes. I made it myself. She clutches it.

"Dada, Dada," she calls.

Father goes over, picks Sarah up, gives her a kiss, and settles her on the blanket. "You go to sleep now,

Sarahle," he says. She curls up, contented, her thumb in her mouth. Then he points to some of the forms on his desk.

"These are admission forms. I don't know how many we'll need. Here's a list of names; I just made them up. Fill out these forms, choosing different times of admission—say, over the last two weeks. We'll pretend you and Mother and Stefan are new admissions. I've put you all in the psychiatric wing. It's empty now."

"What about Sarah?"

"She can stay with us—unless there's a raid. Then she must go into the children's ward."

The "us" he uses isn't lost on me.

"You too, Father?"

"Of course, me too. I can't continue to work here. Now, everyone on the fourth floor knows we're coming. We'll just have to pray there are no traitors in the hospital. This isn't something we can keep secret from the staff. In fact, almost everyone is helping in one way or another. Let's get to work."

I pull up a chair and begin filling out forms. Time drags by, and still Stefan and Mother have not arrived. Finally, at around five, Father takes Sarah and me up to the ward. There are already about thirty other people there, whole families, single people, young, old. Some of them look familiar—

Erik walks in just behind us.

"Erik!" I say with relief. "You came."

"When I went to get my dad at the shipyard, two German transport ships were pulling in. Empty. They're sitting now, waiting, and the guys at the yard say there's no cargo booked for them. The guys have heard the rumor about the roundup and they told Dad to go home, to get Mom, and to hide somewhere. Some of them offered to put us up. Dad just laughed and said he'd see them when he came back to work after Rosh Hashanah. So Dad and I went home, and he and Mom and I talked it over. He says it's hysteria. He doesn't believe we're in danger. He says we're Danes, and they can't take one Dane without taking them all. I wanted to stay, too, but Mom almost pushed me out the door. She won't leave him, but she wouldn't let me stay. The whole thing is really stupid."

Father sighs. "I'll go over there tonight, Erik. I'll try to talk some sense into them."

"He's probably right," Erik says. "After all, the ships could be there for any number of reasons."

"Mother! Stefan!" I call. They are walking down the hallway. I am so glad to see them. "What kept you?"

"Well," says Mother, "we had a lot of people to speak to. We wouldn't come until we'd warned everyone we could think of. David," she adds, "have you been in touch with my brother?"

"Yes," he replies, "just after I spoke to Lisa. He told me he was going to pay a visit to the minister of the church before going on holiday."

"Oh, yes," says Mother, "they're good friends. I hope he can help Poul." She's wringing her hands.

Soon meals are brought up to us all. I wonder how they make hospital food taste so awful. I try to share my *frikadeller* and potatoes with Sarah, but she's not interested. I don't blame her. This food makes even a bottle of warm milk look really good.

Sarah and Mother and I have to stay in one section of the ward, Father and Stefan and Erik in another. Father goes out, as he said he would, but he returns without Erik's parents. Adam won't budge. I pray it's not true and they won't be caught.

It's getting dark out. Many other people have arrived. Two of my friends are here with their families, many acquaintances. Some are crying quietly. Some are white with fear. The nurse had to give sedatives to many. Everyone is terrified. If the Germans find us here, we'll be dragged off and dumped into those ships and then—no one will be able to help us. No one.

I can't sleep. The lights are so bright. I sit or lie here all night, on my cot, thinking back over the past few years, wondering if these will be my last memories. Mother has let me sleep with Sarah. Sarah is my only comfort, but also my greatest burden. Could they kill a little baby like her?

I know they could. And they want to. They want to. They want us all dead.

FOURTEEN

Flight

It's now Sunday night. We've been here for two days. No one talks much. I think if this goes on much longer, we really will be psychiatric patients.

The raids started Friday night, when the Germans thought they'd catch everyone at home celebrating the New Year, and went on most of Saturday.

I know the resistance is trying to arrange a way for us all to get to Sweden. They'll have to smuggle us out of Copenhagen first. The harbor here is full of German ships and patrol boats. They'll have to take us out to the coast. Then if we're lucky it'll be a half-hour crossing to Sweden, but if we have to go south it could take hours. And how are they going to get so many of us out of the city without our being caught?

I feel so sorry for Erik. When one of the doctors

came in and told us that it was true, that all our homes had been raided, Erik sort of fell apart. He'd spent so much time hiding from the truth that he couldn't handle it. He ran around, screamed, cried for his parents. It took Stefan and two others to hold him down while the nurses injected him with a sedative.

Now he just sits in a corner by himself, muttering. When I try to approach him, he turns all red and looks away. He feels humiliated because he was so wrong about everything, and I think he somehow connects me with his shame. But I don't blame him. I really don't. I even sympathize with him for not wanting to face facts. After all, who could find this easy to believe?

This morning thirty more Jews arrived—in the strangest way. I looked out my window and saw a long funeral procession moving toward the chapel in the hospital. The people disappeared inside, and about twenty minutes later all these black-shrouded mourners were being ushered into our ward. Before I was twelve I used to go to Jewish School once a week, and I quickly recognized one of the girls from my class.

"Lissen," I said, catching her hand. "Are you all right?"

She's a petite, dark girl, just my age.

"I'm alive. I suppose that's something," she said.

"Where did you hide?" I asked.

"With some friends. There were lots of us staying at different places in the same neighborhood. But my brother Arthur is an intern here, and he knew there was still room, so he arranged this. We must have walked right by a hundred German soldiers. Arthur says just the fact that we could pull off this funeral charade shows how different Danes are from the German soldiers. If they were ordered to walk through a wall, they would. They can follow orders, but we have imagination." And she actually grinned.

I had to grin back. Here the Germans were, desperately looking for their Jews—Father says he heard that only a few hundred Jews out of eight thousand have been captured so far—and there Lissen and the others are, walking right by them, under their very noses.

"Come sit down with me," I said, "and tell me all about it."

Lissen and I have spent lots of time together since then—we've talked, we've remembered together. The two of us and ten other girls all had our bat mitzvah ceremony together at the synagogue only ten days before the invasion. We were so happy. We all wore white dresses, with white sashes, white stockings, and white shoes. We each read from the prayer Eisheth Hayil. My Hebrew name is Leah, so I read the lines that began with those Hebrew letters. The rabbi blessed us all, and then each family went home and the rabbi visited us one by one. We had a huge feast, and Mother prepared all my favorites: fish with *remoulade* sauce, roast duck, cucumber salad, red cabbage, and for dessert wienerbrød and chocolate cake with fresh whipped cream. The rabbi couldn't eat with us, of course. It wasn't exactly kosher, and anyway, if he did he'd never make it to everyone's house. My bat mitzvah. Now I was a grown woman, an adult. I was so happy. Uncle Poul and Auntie Esther sent me a telegram, my first telegram. Just a week before the invasion—

"Everybody get ready to leave." Suddenly a nurse is standing in the doorway. "Prepare the children. They must all have injections so they'll stay quiet. Put on your warm clothes."

My stomach turns over, then sinks. I run to the bathroom and throw up everything we've eaten that day. When I return I see the nurse injecting Sarah, and I watch as she goes limp in Mother's arms. It's terrible to see her lying there like that. I dress quickly in warm stockings, a woolen skirt, and a thick sweater.

"Everybody downstairs, please," says the nurse. Why do they always have to sound so efficient?

I glance at Lissen. She's across the room with her family. She winks as if to say, "Come on, this'll be an adventure."

We all file downstairs, Stefan and Father joining us. Somehow we have to keep the family together. A long line of ambulances is parked outside the hospital. Groups of fifteen or so pile into each ambulance. One leaves every five minutes. We are in about the third group to go. I don't know anyone in the ambulance other than my family.

"Father, where's Erik?"

"I saw him get into an ambulance up ahead, Lisa. Don't worry."

We ride along silently. I am near the back window. The curtains are drawn, and I don't dare try to open them. Every time we stop I hold my breath, waiting for that awful German voice screaming, "Out." Everyone is silent. The ride seems to go on and on and on.

Finally we stop for good. The doors are opened. We are on a road not far from the coast. "Out, out, hurry," says the driver.

We all scramble out and into the bushes.

"You must hide here," says the driver. "The boats will be along soon. We've arranged payment—don't worry about that. But the Germans are patrolling here on foot, so you may not hear them coming. Be careful. When you hear three low whistles, come down to the water."

I've never been so scared in my life. Not even on our sabotage missions.

My mother drags me along. Father's holding Sarah, who is still fast asleep. Stefan is helping others find places to hide in the bushes. It's cold, and a light rain is falling.

Someone is coming! I hold my breath. Two German soldiers crash through the brush, pointing flashlights everywhere. By some miracle, they see no one and continue on.

All is quiet. Perhaps an hour passes, maybe more. I can't sit here anymore doing nothing. I decide to go and find Stefan. I think I saw him just behind the clump of trees to my right. I stand up and listen, then freeze. There are trucks driving down the road. The sound is loud, there must be lots of them—probably a convoy of German troops being brought out to the countryside to patrol the coastline. They pass us without stopping. I realize I've stopped breathing. I gulp in the cold night air.

I hear some muffled sounds coming from the trees where Stefan is hiding. Then, suddenly, someone is screaming. It's a loud, wild, chilling kind of scream—full of pain—and it sounds like a man. I run toward the sound, my mother calling me back. I find Stefan. He is holding a flashlight on the scene. The scene. An image in my mind, branded there forever. A young man—I know him, he's one of Father's researchers—is standing over the bodies of his wife and his little girl, maybe six, and his little boy, maybe four. Their throats are cut. The man has a bad cut on his neck, too, the blood is all over his collar, but he can't seem to finish what he started.

"It's better for them than being captured," he cries. "We promised each other—" Then he starts to scream again, dropping the knife to the ground.

The driver of the ambulance we rode in has returned. He runs up to the man and holds his arms while Stefan shoves a handkerchief into his mouth to stop the screaming. I take my hanky out, run up, and tie it around the man's neck to slow the bleeding. The man slumps into the driver's arms. He's fainted.

"Something's happened to the boats," the driver says to us. "There's a summerhouse on the other side of the road, at the top of the hill. You'll all have to stay there until we get this straightened out." He gestures toward the three bodies. "I'll take care of this. I'll take them back to Copenhagen with me."

I guess some of the ambulances went to another part of the coast. There seem to be only about thirty of us scrambling through the brush, then across the road and up the hill. The driver has a key and lets us into the house. The people who live here must be helping the resistance. We all hurry into the living room, Stefan and two other young men carrying the bleeding body of the researcher. Father tends to him. I have taken Sarah from Father and hug her as hard as I can. She starts to wake up. When she opens her eyes, she gives me a big smile. The eyes of the researcher's children were wide open, too, surprised. Did their mother hold them, so their father could. . . ?

I start to shiver and my teeth chatter, and I can't seem to stop.

FIFTEEN

The Soldier

It's cold, dark, and quiet—very quiet. Stefan knows the driver of the van and has found out from him that the fisherman who was to take us suddenly demanded huge sums of money. The resistance is trying to find the money or some other fisherman who will take us over for a reasonable amount. In the meantime we have to wait.

Fishing boats are the only boats the Germans have allowed us to keep in the water, so I can see it will be up to the fishermen to transport the thousands of refugees. Stefan says a lot of people arranged their own passage to Sweden on the first day after the roundup—mostly by getting fishermen to take them—but it wasn't easy to set up, and some of them got caught. So now the resistance is organizing the rescue. I hope Erik is all right. He must be with another group.

"Lisa?"

It's Stefan.

"Yes?"

"How well can you use a gun?"

"I'm not as good as Susanne, but I know how to shoot one. You know that."

"The boat is ready to take this group," he says.

"Oh, thank God."

"But I've been told that more people will be using this place as a drop-off point, some tonight, some tomorrow night. They need people to patrol the area, to watch for Germans, you know. I've volunteered to stay and help. I'll go over on the last boat tomorrow. After that they'll make the drops somewhere else for a while."

I can't believe Stefan is actually asking me to stay with him. You'd think he'd force me onto that boat.

"My orders are to give you the choice of going or staying."

Everything in the resistance is more tightly controlled now, since martial law was imposed. The resistance is sort of like a government in itself, with each cell responsible to the one above it. Heading it all is the Freedom Council, made up of seven resistance leaders. I have no idea who Stefan's contact is—he'd never tell me. Anyway, I know better than to ask. But obviously it's someone who knows me.

A million things run through my mind—Sweden,

safety, Mother, Father, Sarah, the night, the fear—and yet, when I open my mouth, I surprise myself.

"I'll stay."

Stefan shakes his head impatiently. "I knew you'd say that. Listen, Lisa, you should go. Mother and Father and Sarah need you, too. You know how dangerous this is."

"Then why are you staying?" I ask.

"Because someone has to."

I try to give him a knowing look, but it doesn't work because it's pitch black.

"Well, there you are," I say finally.

"And I can just imagine the expression on your face," he sighs. "Let's help get this group on its way. You're to stay near the road. If you see any vehicles, give one low whistle. If any stop or slow down, two short. All clear is three short."

"Good thing you taught me to whistle, big brother."

He musses my hair. "Be careful!" he cautions.

"Don't worry. I won't give them the satisfaction of capturing one extra Jew."

"No, neither will I," he says.

I step over feet and bodies, sometimes tripping, whispering my father's name until I get a response. I find his hand. My mother finds mine. I take a deep breath and brace myself before I begin.

"I'm staying behind until the last boat," I tell them.

"No, Lisa," they say together, "you certainly are not!"

"Someone has to." I try to sound calm and in control,

when really I feel like throwing up again. I don't think I have anything left in my stomach, though.

"Lisa," says Father sternly, "I forbid it."

"Father," I plead, "don't say that. I know how to use a gun. I've been on underground missions before. They need me. It could be little Sarah I help save."

To my complete shock, Mother interjects. "Let her decide, David. She's not a little girl anymore. My God, I wish she were. But she's old enough to make up her own mind."

"But why not one of us?" says my father. "I'll go in her place. I have more experience. . . ."

"They need you on the boat, dear. You'll have to inject the children again, keep everyone calm—and what if we run into trouble on the water? We need people on the boat who can help, too." She pauses. "Lisa," she says, "you must decide, but I think you've done more than enough to help. At some point you must think of yourself and your family." I can hear her voice breaking. "We couldn't bear to lose you." She pauses again. "What does Stefan say?"

"Stefan is staying, too."

Now they are both silent. It is too much for them.

I throw my arms around them and give them each a big hug. Then Sarah a kiss. I move away, through the dark, before they can stop me.

Some flashlights are turned on. I see parents taking their children to Father for more injections. Suddenly one of the children starts to cry. No, to scream. She's hysterical. Then another starts. And another. Soon the entire house is filled with the sound of screaming, frantic children. I can hear Sarah crying, too. I can tell she's scared. But Father is working quickly to get them all quiet.

Stefan comes up behind me, touching my arm.

"Let's get outside," he says. "My contact is waiting. If the Germans don't hear this, it'll be a miracle."

The injections should work soon, I think. If only there are no patrols in the area.

I follow Stefan's flashlight beam outside. A figure is waiting for us in the dark. He hands me a gun. I feel it. It's a handgun with a silencer. I know it's not a Danish gun. Our homemade ones are twice as big and heavy.

"We're getting good supplies in from England these days," says a familiar voice.

"Hi, Jesper," I say quietly.

"I'm glad you're going to be with us, Lisa."

His words run up and down my spine, making me shiver.

"Cold?" asks my dumb brother.

"No, I'm fine," I say. "Where do I go?"

"You and I will scout down to the waterfront," says Jesper. "Stefan will stay here, watching. When he hears our all clear, he'll bring everyone down."

"All clear is three short whistles," Stefan reminds me.

"Right," says Jesper. "In about an hour there'll be another lot of people arriving, so we should all stay down near the water after the first boat leaves."

At that, keeping his beam very low, he starts down the hill. I follow him closely.

It's becoming quiet now, and the babies' crying is

dying down. By the time we get to the road, there is complete silence. The road is empty. We scramble down to the water's edge. There's a large fishing boat sitting a little way out from the shore. We can see the lights of Sweden twinkling in the distance, perhaps thirty or forty minutes' boat ride away. This is a good spot.

Suddenly I hear loud footsteps and voices talking in German. I reach out to Jesper. He turns off his flashlight. We crouch down. I hear him click the safety off and put his gun on half cock. I do the same. They are close to us now; they have stopped for a cigarette. One of them says he's going to check the waterfront. He must not be allowed to see the boat.

Jesper whispers in my ear, "I'll go around and take care of the other one. The one going to the water is yours." I squeeze his wrist to let him know I hear and understand, that I know what I must do. I can't think about it—I must just do it.

Like a cat, Jesper makes his way back toward the road. A solitary German soldier walks within a few feet of me. I follow, treading softly, using the trees for cover. Within a minute he is standing on the beach, looking at the fishing trawler. My heart is pounding. My hand is sweating so much I can hardly hold the gun. I move out from behind the tree, kneel, rest the gun on my left arm as I've been taught, aim carefully. The soldier turns to call to his friend.

Pop. The sound comes from behind me—Jesper has done his part. *Pop*. My gun goes off, too. The German shrieks, then falls over. He's screaming horribly. I run toward him. I hear someone behind me. I turn and see a dark shape. I'm sure it's Jesper. He comes up beside me; we reach the German at the same time. The German has his gun out of his holster and is pointing it at us. It's too dark to see his face clearly. Jesper fires. The gun drops from the German's hand. He lies there, silent. Jesper whistles three times.

"Come and help me with the other one. They'll both have to go on the boat, on a halfway ticket," says Jesper. I run with him, following his beam. The other soldier is shot neatly through the head.

I can't help myself. I go and retch in the bushes. It makes me feel even worse. When I come back, Jesper runs a hand over my forehead. Then he puts his arms around me and holds me, tight, for just a minute. I'm shaking badly. He kisses me lightly on the forehead, then lets me go. He grabs the German's arms, I take his legs, and we drag him over to his comrade.

Within minutes the people from the house are scrambling through the bushes toward the beach. The children are all being carried; they are unconscious. On a signal from Jesper the trawler comes in as close as it can. Everyone wades into the water. Rowboats are sent to shore, and everyone climbs in and they're rowed to the trawler and helped aboard. Jesper and Stefan carry the dead soldiers to a rowboat. We can't afford to have their bodies found. I stay in the background. I know that if my parents saw me now, they'd drag me along.

As soon as Jesper and Stefan are back on land, I hear the motor of the boat starting up. Slowly it moves away, toward Sweden and safety. I think of Sarah lying drugged in my mother's arms, of Mother and Father looking back through the dark, wishing, wishing Stefan and I were with them. I try not to think of the possibility that the boat may be stopped by the Germans, that everyone on board could be captured.

SIXTEEN

Stefan and Jesper and I

The trawler is gone and the two of us huddle together under a tree, taking shelter from the light rain. We are waiting for the next load of people and the next boat.

"I think it's time for us to scout around," says Jesper, "and make sure there are no more patrols."

"Why are we using this place as a drop when it's so heavily patrolled?" I ask.

"It wasn't heavily patrolled yesterday," he answers. "The Germans are probably moving around to cover as much of the coast as they can."

"Well," I retort, "they can't cover all of it, and I think it's too bad we're using the one place they are covering."

"Lisa," Stefan explains, "they'll be patrolling all up

and down the coast. But they'll be spreading themselves thin. Probably there won't be replacements for those two, so nobody will notice they're missing for at least twenty-four hours. That should give us the time we need."

"I hope so," I whisper.

"Let's spread out along the road," says Jesper, "and watch for the new arrivals."

"You and I can split up," Stefan agrees, "but I think Lisa should stay with me for a bit."

I don't object. The shooting has left me shaken, terrified of having to do it again.

We separate from Jesper and go up near the empty road, by the trees. It's about two A.M.

Suddenly I see car lights.

"What's that?" I whisper.

Stefan peers down the road, then steps out and beams his flashlight.

"A taxi," he says.

"A taxi?"

It stops and lets out five people. They are looking around, terrified, helpless. The three of us run to them and lead them away from the road, into the bushes and trees.

For the next half hour a taxi stops every five minutes. Six taxis in all. There are four to six people in each car. Finally they're all here, and out on the water I can see two trawlers moving slowly toward us. Jesper flashes his beam on the water, turning it on and off twice. The boats return the signal. We hustle the people into the water, old, young, parents carrying drugged children. Like the first trawler, these boats are too big to come into shallow water, so they send little rowboats. People clamber into the rowboats, mothers and fathers carrying infants, old people being helped by the strong young ones, until finally they are all in the boats. We can hear the oars hitting the water as the boats are rowed out to the trawlers. Quietly the engines of the trawlers start, and they are off.

The three of us look at each other and grin. This time it has all gone off without a hitch.

"We can go up to the house now," says Jesper. "That's it for tonight. We'll start again tomorrow night. You're to be on the last boat," he says to me.

"What about you?" I say to him.

"Not me. I can still be of help here."

He leads us up to the house and we let ourselves in. We can't turn on the lights, but we can use the bathroom—and then the beds.

I climb into what must be a child's bed, covered with a beautiful thick comforter. And I sink into it, into the warmth. I have no time to think. I drift and then I sleep.

When I wake up, I'm alone. I'm in a cozy little room done up with bright blue flowered wallpaper. A small wooden horse stands in the corner. There are shelves of children's books beside the bureau. It's a wonderful, safe place, and I don't feel like getting out of bed. I force myself to, however, and go into a large, sunny living room. Jesper and Stefan are drinking coffee at the long dining-room table. The room is bright, even with the curtains drawn.

"Oh, I'd like some of that," I say, "unless Stefan made it."

"I did," he retorts, insulted, "and just for that, you can't have any."

I look in the pot. "There isn't any left."

"Just what I said," he repeats. "Can't have any."

I find my way to the kitchen, not deigning to reply. I won't sink to his level.

There's real coffee—I brew a whole pot! We've been using chicory for ages now, ever since coffee started to be rationed. I take the fresh pot and a cup and return to the dining room. When I sit down at the table and take my first sip, I think I'm in heaven.

Jesper is smiling at me. Suddenly I realize how dreadful I must look, unwashed, muddy. I put my hand to my hair; it's full of twigs and dirt and is in a complete tangle.

"You look as though you're in heaven," he says.

I smile back. I guess under the circumstances I can be excused for being slightly messy.

"That's how I feel. Or I would if Stefan weren't here—what would he be doing in heaven?"

Stefan snorts. "Well, this may not be heaven, little sister, but tonight you're going to Sweden. That should be the next best thing."

"What do you mean, *I'm* going to Sweden? What about you?"

"Well . . ." Stefan pauses.

"Oh, Stefan!" I exclaim, "you can't be thinking of staying."

"He's thinking of it," says Jesper, "but he can't. High command says he must go. It's too dangerous to allow any Jews to stay. Besides, he can't be of any use anymore."

Stefan jumps up and begins to pace. "I don't want to go. Why should I? It's my country, and I'm going to stay and fight."

"And I'm going to get you on that ship if I have to carry you on," says Jesper firmly.

"And I'll help you," I add. "Stefan, you endanger other people by staying. They'll catch you. And what if they torture you? What if something slips—"

"I've thought of that," he says, and reaches into his pocket. He brings out something in his closed fist. Slowly he opens his hand. I see a small white pill. One single, small, white, round pill. I know what it is—Father showed them to me when we were in the hospital. Cyanide. I feel paralyzed. I can't move. I can't speak.

"Stefan," says Jesper, "if you stay you'll have to use that pill. And the Germans will have won another victory. Please, be reasonable. I'm sure there'll be things you can do from Sweden. Perhaps they can even use you in London. Maybe they'll give you a disguise, new papers, and drop you back in. But in the meantime, listen to them, get out now."

Jesper looks at the little pill. I wonder if he carries one—so quick, so easy.

"All right, Jesper," Stefan says quietly. "I'll think about it."

I just sit there. Even my coffee won't go down properly. All I can see is that little white pill in Stefan's hand.

It's hard to believe we've been driven to this. Stefan—so young, so handsome, so smart, with so much ahead of him—sitting at a stranger's table, in his own country, staring at a little white pill. Some Jews have used them already, Father told me, rather than be captured. Some who might have escaped used them instead, too scared to try anything else, and some who were captured used them, too. I can't stop seeing it. I think of Stefan using it. I feel as though somehow, if I look at that pill long enough, I'll understand the war, that this is what the war is all about—that little white pill.

SEVENTEEN

Good-bye

We have spent the day, the three of us, sitting around, talking, telling stories, recalling close calls and funny episodes. Jesper told us of the time he was ordered to kill a collaborator. This man was a big industrialist with lots of friends. Jesper just waited for him at the top of the stairs that led to his apartment, then shot him.

Jesper ran away and no one caught him, but it was at the beginning of the war—he was inexperienced, he was young. He wanted to go to the funeral and ended up going with Stefan. They saw all those people standing around saying what a good man the industrialist had been. Jesper said the man must have caused the arrest, directly, of at least twenty Danes. But of course, the Germans were there, too. And when the boys walked out of the cemetery, a big black Gestapo car was waiting, and the Gestapo officer pointed at the two of them and they were ordered into the car. They were questioned for about twenty minutes.

Why were they there?

Just interested.

Why were they interested?

Oh, you know—important man dies, you like to pay your respects.

Why?

Why not?

And on, and on.

Finally, the Gestapo officer let them go. But Jesper said that as they walked away, the Germans' guns at their backs, he'd never been so sure he was about to die. He could feel the bullet going in, hear the gunfire start. Stefan laughed. He, too, was waiting for that shot in the back. But it never came. The Gestapo never even took down their names. . . .

We have managed to fix ourselves a pretty fair lunch, then dinner, using the tins stored in the cupboards, although I take it easy on the food—just more to throw up later—and the day has gone quickly. I love sitting and talking with these two. But now it's time.

We ready our guns. I hold my gun in one hand, my flashlight in the other. We leave the house. It's been quiet all day, and now there are no signs of German patrols. There is no moon. Like last night, a light rain is falling.

Within half an hour our first load of people arrives: a dairy truck filled with Jewish families. Quickly we unload them and take them down to the water. There are about fifteen people. Three motorboats are waiting. They wade out to the boats and leave.

The driver of the dairy van talks to us. "Just one more drop," he says. "It's too risky now because it seems a couple of German soldiers are missing around here. Just one more small group coming. A trawler should be here at exactly eleven o'clock."

He leaves. It is ten-thirty. My skin starts to crawl. I don't know why.

At ten-fifty two ambulances stop at the roadside. The hospitals all over Copenhagen must be helping. About thirty people get out. Some of them I know. They are glad to see a familiar face, but a friend of my mother's starts to bawl me out.

"This is no work for a young girl, Lisa. Your poor mother must be worried sick. Now you stop this nonsense and get on the boat."

"I will, I will, Mrs. Abramsen," I assure her. "I'm just helping people. I'll be on the boat with you."

Her daughter, a thirteen-year-old I know, is looking at me as though I'm a crazy person or something. Maybe I am.

The big trawler is out in the water. We signal and it sends two rowboats in. We put the people in the boats. There's room for almost everyone. About five have to stay behind.

"Tell them to send a boat back again," says Stefan. About ten minutes go by. Jesper, Stefan, and I are listening and looking for any German patrols. Finally a rowboat returns, rowed by a young man who looks as though he belongs to the fishing trawler. Mrs. Abramsen gets in, her daughter, her husband, their nine-year-old boy, a young woman of about thirty, then myself, and, thank God, Stefan. I didn't know until he put his foot in the boat whether he'd be sensible.

Jesper wades into the water with us, gives Stefan a big hug—almost tips the boat—then reaches for me, practically pulls me into the water, and kisses me—I mean a real kiss. Then we're rowing away, and Jesper is back in the bushes. And Stefan, for once, keeps his wisecracks to himself.

Suddenly a bright beam of light comes from the east, over the water. The trawler starts its motor and heads west, lights off, as fast as it can go.

Stefan picks up the other oar. He and the young man start to row as hard as they can, west, into the shallow water.

"They should pass us without seeing us," whispers the young man. "But I'm afraid they've spotted the trawler." They have. Sirens are blaring; they are firing warning shots.

"It may be all right," he says to us. "We've put everyone under the coal, in the bottom of the boat. The captain may talk himself out of it."

Is that gunfire I hear on shore? I find myself praying.

Dear God, don't let anything happen to Jesper.

But why should He listen? It's silly to pray like that. He hasn't listened for all the others who've been captured, who've died. I make myself stop.

Jesper, I say to myself, be careful. Take care of yourself.

We are rowing through the black, inky night. We will have to row all the way to Sweden. What should have been a quick trip will now take hours. If we get there at all—for the rain is becoming heavy, and we can no longer see the lights. After a while I row for Stefan. I'm strong, and the young woman rows, too. Then Stefan and Hans, the young man from the fishing trawler, take over again. We don't talk. Mrs. Abramsen tries to keep her children calm and quiet. She whispers stories to them about what life will be like in Sweden. It's so black, so lonely out here. Will we ever get there? Perhaps we're going in circles. Perhaps we'll end up back in Denmark. My feet feel wetter than the rest of me. I look down. The boat is leaking.

"This boat wasn't built for a trip like this, and with so many people," says Hans. We try to bail the water out with our hands, but more and more is coming in.

"Jonathan is only nine," says Mrs. Abramsen. "He can swim. But not so far. And where, which way do we swim?" Her daughter starts to cry. The boat is sinking lower and lower.

Suddenly a big bright white light bears down on us. We all gasp in fright. There is no escape. The white light gets brighter and brighter; the ship is getting closer and closer. The waves from the huge vessel are rocking our little boat. We rock, the water comes in, and suddenly we are all floundering in the water.

"Jonathan, Jonathan," I hear his father call to him.

Oh, it's cold! It's so cold. Shall I just let myself go under? Wouldn't that be better than a slow death in a concentration camp or a quick one in a gas chamber?

Better to end it now. It's so noisy, the ship must be huge. There's a lifesaver thrown just in front of me. I see Jonathan floundering. I go to him, drag him to the lifesaver. "Hang on," I say, "they'll pull you up." But why not let him drown, too? The others are all catching hold of lifesavers. I see a flash in my mind, a small white pill; would it dissolve in water? I swim, calling for Stefan in the black water. I can hear voices above us; the others are being hauled out of the water. I see Stefan, swim over to him.

He knows. He grips my shoulder. "Don't worry," he says. "It dissolved. I didn't have a chance."

A lifesaver is dropped to us and Stefan puts my arms over it. He hangs on with me, knowing I won't go without him. Slowly, slowly, we're pulled out, up, water dripping from us, teeth chattering, bodies shaking. Hands reach out for us and pull us onto the deck. Then a warm smile, a handshake. The captain of the ship saying, "Welcome to Sweden. Welcome to Sweden."

I look at Stefan. The captain is shaking his hand. Stefan's face is breaking out in a big broad smile. We look around us. A Swedish destroyer. As good as Swedish soil. Tears are flowing down my face, but I'm so wet I hardly notice them.

"Welcome to Sweden."

I look back toward Denmark. The only words that could sound sweeter would be "Welcome home."

And I know I will live to hear them.

AFTERWORD

The Holocaust—Hitler's systematic destruction of European Jewry—killed about six million Jews and virtually exterminated the Jewish culture throughout the lands occupied by Germany.

Because of the courage and resourcefulness shown by the Danish people, both Jews and gentiles, Denmark was one small bright corner in that terrible time. Of some 7,000 Danish Jews, only 474 were arrested and sent to the concentration camp of Theresienstadt, while the rest escaped to the safety of neutral Sweden.

But this great escape could not have happened if the SS had succeeded in trapping families in their homes on Rosh Hashanah, the Jewish New Year. That shameful plan was foiled by G. F. Duckwitz, the member of the German embassy staff who was in charge of shipping in Copenhagen. Duckwitz risked his own life, first by trying unsuccessfully to prevent the roundup and then by secretly passing on a warning.

Carol Matas always dreamed of becoming an actress. In fact, her writing career began by accident when her acting career was on hiatus. She began writing stories as a hobby and reading them to her friends. She now writes full time, gives workshops and readings, and always has about three different ideas for new books circulating in her head. Carol lives in Winnipeg, Manitoba.

Lisa was awarded the Geoffrey Bilson Award for Historical Fiction for Young People and named an Honor Book for Young Adults by the Sydney Taylor Book Award Committee.